Enforcer

~The Crime and Passion Stalk City Hall Series~

By

Valerie J. Clarizio

Donna,
Enjoy!
Valerie J. Clarizio

THE CODE ENFORCER

~Crime and Passion Stalk City Hall Series~

First edition. November 2018.

Published by *VJC Books*, 2018

ISBN-13: 978-1096461234

Written by Valerie J. Clarizio.

Dedication

To all the hardworking local government employees.
Thank you for all you do!

Chapter One

Investigator Markie Pearson covered her nose and mouth with the tissue balled in her hand as she squeezed between the piled newspapers, magazines, and plastic food containers stacked floor to ceiling in the enclosed porch. Sister Ann was a hoarder all right.

Markie kept her limbs tucked in in an effort to not touch any of the germ-infested filth, or more importantly, risk contaminating the crime scene.

Just ahead, stood a rusty, old upright freezer. Judging from the atrocious odor bringing tears to her eyes, she guessed the old lady had been locked in there for a while. Would have been better—smelled less vile—had the freezer been plugged in.

She blinked rapidly and then patted her eyes with her sleeve as she leaned over some garbage to get a better look at the body partially hanging out of the freezer. According to Officer Blart, the woman had been fully tucked into the appliance until Bryce Hawk, the City Planner and Zoning/Property Maintenance Administrator, bumped into it when a few rotting deck boards gave way beneath his feet.

Needing a closer look, she stepped gingerly over the broken planks holding hope the remaining boards would support her weight.

Involuntarily, her nose scrunched up. Yep, the body had definitely been there for a few days or so. The deceased's fingertips and toes were near black in color.

If Bryce hadn't done the court ordered thirty-day check on Sister Ann's property, it would be hard to tell when her body would have been discovered. Markie thought for a moment, did it matter? Two days or twenty days, dead was dead.

Now, for the bigger questions, who in the hell would stuff an eighty-year-old lady into an upright, unplugged freezer on an enclosed back porch? Was the woman already dead when she got locked in there, or did she die in the freezer?

The rundown home indicated Sister Ann didn't have two nickels to rub together, and there was likely nothing of value in the house—so a robbery motive was probably out. Plus, from what Bryce had previously told her, the place was loaded with garbage. When he and the firefighters inspected the home in the past, they had limited access by narrow pathways lined with newspapers, cardboard boxes, and plastic butter and whip cream containers. In some instances, they actually had to climb over debris to get to a room. If not for the fact the nun fell one day, and Father Dennis happened to find her and called 9-1-1, the first responders would have never seen the overabundance of debris in her home. They reported it as a health hazard, the city investigated, and eventually a court order was issued to Sister Ann to clean up the house. Yep, robbery was out—too much work in this case to find anything of value.

The fact this woman was a nun, and retired Catholic school principal, led Markie to believe she probably hadn't screwed anyone over in her life to warrant a revenge murder. Then again, maybe she rapped on some kid's knuckles one too many times with a wooden ruler.

She shook her head. The city had dealt with hoarders in the past, but this one took the cake. As she understood it, Sister had been issued a court order to clear out the debris. At first, she flat-out refused, but then warmed up a bit to the idea with some coaxing by Fire Chief Bosley. Perhaps the rumors about the flirtatious fire chief were true—he could even charm the panties off a nun.

Markie stifled her giggle and regained her composure. Sister's death was no laughing matter.

The next breath she pulled in sent the contents of her stomach swirling, forcing her to spin around and head for the door, leaving the evidence technician alone to do his thing.

Once outside, she gulped in a fresh breath of oxygen. The hot, humid air almost melted her lungs, but anything was better than the flavor of rotting flesh that clung to her taste buds. A few more long, slow intakes of air cleared her burning nostrils. The horrid smell of a days old dead body was bad enough, but to add a ninety-degree, humid day increased it tenfold.

"That's some awful smelling shit in there, huh?" Kent Urban yelled to her from where he stood over by the leaning, detached, one stall garage.

He wasn't kidding, but was he talking about all the crap in the house or Sister Ann's body?

Markie swung her gaze from Kent to the man next to him—Bryce Hawk. She eyed his six- pack abs. Why on earth wasn't he wearing a shirt? Scanning over him she noted he wore his other usual work attire—dress pants and shoes, but no shirt. Her gaze bounced back up to the man's broad chest. *Nice. Too nice.*

Being a firefighter and first responder for at least ten years or so already, Kent was probably used to this kind of stuff by now, but the tall, muscular man standing next to him, the one whose skin tone held a blue hue obviously wasn't. The city planner wore blue well. In fact, he wore everything well. Problem was he knew it, and every woman between the age of eighteen and eighty knew it. The man reminded her so much of her cheating ex-fiancé she could hardly stand to look at him. It wasn't necessarily his looks that resembled Conner, but his actions. He was a smooth talker. Yet, he was so damn handsome she couldn't help gawking.

Even in consideration of the unusual Wisconsin ninety-degree temperature, Markie's body heat rose a few degrees when Bryce's dark gaze scanned over her as she walked toward him. *Dammit.* She hated being affected by a womanizer this way, but something about him got to her, and she had a tough time ignoring it.

She shifted her focus to Kent. "I see the fire department's volunteer efforts to help declutter Sister's house didn't go very far."

He shook his head. "We took a dumpster load out of the house last month, and all she did was refill the house fuller than it was prior to that. How on earth does she get all this garbage?"

"Good question. I don't know. But she won't be any longer."

Markie slid her gaze to the dark-eyed man next to her. His irises were almost as black as his thick, wavy hair. She was dying to ask him why he wasn't wearing a shirt, but then, the rotten, bodily juices stench from his direction hit her like a punch to the gut, and she burst out laughing.

"Don't tell me the corpse fell onto you?"

Bryce shook his head. "It's not funny. That putrid smell will forever be embedded in my nostrils, and I need to get the hell out of here to shower. When can I go?"

So, the old lady had fallen on top of him when she fell out of the freezer. That had to be why he wasn't wearing a shirt. *Priceless*. This was good stuff.

"This could take some time," Markie replied, working hard to keep her lips from curling into a smile. She planned to keep the arrogant, womanizing guy for a while for questioning, just for fun. Let him wallow in the torture of that awful smell on himself.

Bryce crossed his arms over that appealing broad chest of his cutting off her view, then he shifted from his right foot to the left. He dipped awkwardly like his knee buckled or something. She'd noticed that before; he seemed to favor his left leg. Did the man's perfect body hold an imperfection? Maybe so, judging from the slight limp he displayed on occasion.

A fault. How deserving for a womanizer.

The medical examiner pulled into the driveway, parked, and slipped out of his vehicle. The short, thin man walked up the cracked sidewalk and stepped into the enclosed porch.

"Don't go away. I'll be right back. I need to talk to the ME," Markie said to Bryce.

He blew out an exasperated sigh.

Taking her chances, she placed a foot on the spongy step of the porch. With caution, she took another step and then another until she was standing next to the scrawny man inspecting the nun's body.

With all the junk in the porch, it was amazing someone was able to stuff the woman into the freezer.

"How long do you think she's been there?" Markie asked.

The medical examiner looked over his shoulder and shrugged. "Almost a week, give or take."

"It'll be interesting to know how she died, whether she suffocated in there, or was she dead when someone put her inside? There's no claw marks to indicate she tried to get out. And since the door is only hanging onto its hinges by a thread, and there's no lock, she should have been easily able to push it open."

He nodded. "Time will tell."

Once the funeral home staff arrived, the ME bagged Sister Ann, and he and Officer Blart carried her out. They set her on the gurney, then they slipped her into the hearse.

Markie stared after them as they pulled out of sight. Who on earth would do this to a little old lady—a nun? Who had something to gain from her death?

The answer to the questions hit her like a ton of bricks—Bryce.

She glanced over her shoulder to the shirtless man by the garage. He definitely had something to gain. Sister Ann was nothing but a big headache to the guy. Her property maintenance issue caused him nothing but grief by having to file a ton of paperwork, and follow up every month to see if there were any improvements. Then there was the outcry from the general public he had to deal with. He was the mean old city employee who harassed a poor, little old nun. Of course, the public didn't understand the guy was just doing his job, and the actions he took were really only for the general well-being of the sister and her neighbors.

The death of Sister Ann would make the city planner's life a lot easier.

Yep, the infamous Bryce Hawk was suspect number one.

Chapter Two

Bryce fixed his gaze on the sexy-as-sin investigator as she sashayed toward him. Markie Pearson reached up and flung her wavy, flaming red hair over her shoulders giving him a better look at her attractive, milky-white skin peppered with freckles.

But it was those bright emerald eyes that did him in. He could stare into those alluring irises forever.

Too bad for him those eyes belonged to a woman who detested him for some reason, and a woman he knew he was better off avoiding for his own sake. Markie was the long-term relationship kind—the marrying kind. The two things his father's four divorces had taught him were that long-term relationships were just a pipe dream to those who believed in them, and that the Hawk men were not meant for the long-haul.

Markie halted a few steps away but kept her judging gaze on him. "So, Bryce, tell me exactly what happened when you got here. Step by step."

Between the thought of the sister's dead body falling on top of him, and the stench of death clinging to his skin, he was two swallows away from hurling. He worked to tamp down the bile in his throat.

"I came here to see if she'd made any progress to clean up her house, as per the court order. I used the back door because ever since I've been coming here the front one's been blocked by garbage. I stepped into the breezeway and knocked on the inside door. When she didn't answer, I knocked again. At that point, the floorboards gave way and I grabbed for the freezer. It tilted and the door flew open. I thought it was going to go through the floor too, but it caught on all the crap next to it and didn't. I still lost my balance and fell to the ground, and..." A tremor raked through his body, and he swallowed hard. "Sister fell on top of me."

The glint in Markie's gaze let him know she enjoyed his uneasiness.

Annoyance raked through him. *Why does she feel the need to bask in my discomfort? What did I ever do to her for her to despise me?*

Without conscious thought, he shifted his weight from his right foot to his left. Pain shot through his knee. Instinctively he looked down at his leg while working to disguise his grimace—keep the secret about his leg. If not for that stupid prosthetic leg he probably wouldn't have fallen all the way down, but no, when he twisted as he reached for the freezer it unhinged and he fell hard.

"Before today, when was the last time you were here?" Markie asked drawing his attention back to her.

"A month ago."

"And she was okay then?"

He shrugged. "She was alive."

"So, you had no other *contact* with her from then until today?"

This started to feel like an inquisition. "No."

"Do you know how her body got into the freezer?"

Holy crap. She was questioning him as if he were a suspect.

His pulse raced and his palms perspired. "No, I don't know how she got into the freezer. You think *I* did this?" he asked in a tone a bit higher pitched than usual.

Markie raised her hand. "I'm just trying to figure out what happened here."

"Well, I don't know. I just found her is all. If I had known she was in the freezer I wouldn't have let her fall on me. Last time I was here she was fine." He crossed his arms over his chest. "In fact, Father Dennis was here, too. He tried to convince her to let the firefighters help her clear out some more stuff. The dumpster they'd filled last month hardly made a dent."

"Hmm, I wonder when the last time Father was here." the exasperating woman stated.

"I can check with him," Officer Blart said from behind Markie, then he stepped up to her side. "I just spoke to one of the neighbors and they didn't recall seeing anybody here lately. A week or so ago they saw her hauling bags out of her car and into the house." Blart shook his head. "Like she needs more bags of junk. Where does she get it all?"

Bryce cleared his throat. "Can I go? I really need to shower."

Markie kept her probing gaze on him for a brief moment before she nodded.

So much for that beautiful emerald gaze of hers. It was more irritating now than anything.

He slid into his city vehicle and headed for home—shirtless. The police had taken it for evidence, but it didn't matter anyway because he would have tossed it into the garbage.

What a shit-ass day.

It wasn't even noon yet and he'd been threatened by Junior Willming with a broken handled trenching spade during his first property maintenance check of the day, and then Sister's dead body fell onto him during his second.

Screw it. He wasn't doing the other two checks today. They could wait. It wasn't like any of these people ever complied with the court orders anyway, and in the end, the judge would just slap them on the wrist and give them another thirty days to clean up the mess. Property maintenance was just a joke, a waste of everybody's time, his in particular. God how he hated this part of his job.

Bryce parked his car in his driveway and headed for the front door of his two-story, brick, fixer-upper. Though his dad thought him nuts for buying this old house, he'd fallen in love with it—the potential—the second he saw it.

He pushed through the heavy, wooden front door and made his way past the plaster buckets, down the wide hall, and into the master bathroom. Under the hot spray of the shower, he scrubbed his chest and arm raw to ensure he'd rid himself of the awful fluids and stench that seeped into his skin when the nun fell on him. As long as he lived, that horrendous stench would forever be embedded into his brain.

After a good length of time, he determined if the germs weren't already scrubbed away they never would be. He stepped out of the shower, dried off, and slid into some work clothes, then he padded off to the kitchen to grab a sandwich before returning to work. No more field work for the day, though. He was going to hide in his office and do some menial paperwork for the rest of his shift which would hopefully take his mind off the awful morning he'd had.

Once back at work, it didn't take but five minutes and Markie Pearson knocked on his office door. He didn't care how beautiful she was, she was the last person he wanted to see right now.

Unfortunately, willing her away didn't work.

She stepped in and took a seat on one of the chairs opposite his desk, leaned back, and crossed her arms over her chest. Her judging, emerald gaze bore into him.

Not planning to let her get the best of him, he leaned back and mimicked her.

The woman's gaze softened as the corners of her mouth twitched upward. It was like she enjoyed his discomfort—the horrific morning he'd had. His jaw clenched.

Markie unfolded her arms and leaned forward. "So, it will be interesting to see the preliminary autopsy report on Sister Ann. Hopefully, we'll hear something tomorrow, though we'll have to wait months for the final."

Leaning forward, he rested his elbows on his desk. Why had she told him this? "Okay?"

"Just sayin'. Can you think of anything else you may have seen at Sister's house that looked out of the ordinary?"

"You've seen her house and yard. There's nothing ordinary about it. It's a complete disaster."

Flaming strands of hair shifted slightly as the investigator nodded. "True. The officers are canvassing the neighborhood, and so far, nobody's noticed anyone strange hanging around. Just you."

His heart slammed against his ribcage. Here she went accusing him again. "I was there doing my job."

"Uh, huh."

"What do you mean by uh, huh?"

"Well, you have to admit you have a lot to gain by the death of the nun. As you've said in the past, she's been a thorn in your side. Did you not say that?"

Sweat beaded on his upper lip and temples. He had said that. Probably a hundred times, but it was nothing he didn't say about his other property maintenance issues, too.

"I did say it. But I certainly wouldn't kill her over it. And actually, I have more to gain by her *not* being dead."

One perfectly manicured eyebrow arched. "How so?"

"Job security." Ha, he had her there.

"Or, that could be a nice cover story for you," she shot back.

They stared at each other for a moment. The hint of softness in her gaze told him she didn't really believe he had anything to do with Sister's death, yet she continued to pressure him. Why she detested him he hadn't a clue. They both worked at City Hall and saw each other daily, but didn't communicate with each other much outside of the property maintenance cases, and even then, he worked more with the officers than with her.

Maybe now was the time to get to the bottom of this.

He inched his chair farther under his desk until his stomach pressed against the laminate surface so he could lean closer to the woman opposite him.

It took less than two seconds for him to realize he shouldn't have done that.

Her scent, that sensual hint of coconut that reminded him of sunscreen, drove him crazy. Winter, spring, summer, or fall, she always wore the same scent, so it couldn't really be sunscreen, right? Though, with that fair skin of hers, she probably did have to be cautious in any sunshine, or perhaps even the LED lights hanging from the ceiling.

Mentally, he shook his head. *Dammit, focus.*

"Let's just cut to the chase here about the real reason you're busting my balls," he finally stated.

Markie averted her gaze and shifted in her chair.

Hmm, Ms. Tough As Nails doesn't seem to like this topic.

Time to press further. "I take it I've done something in the past you don't like. Would you care to enlighten me…get it out in the open, so we can resolve the issue?"

The anxious redhead brushed her hands over her thighs then lifted her gaze to meet his. "Don't flatter yourself, nothing you do warrants my attention. I'm just doing my job here. Following up on all leads. And you did find the body, so why wouldn't I question you? How about we just stay focused on the issue at hand here."

Good recovery Markie Pearson, good recovery. But there's more to this story—your story—and I intend to find out what it is.

Chapter Three

Against his better judgement based on the happenings with Sister Ann the day before, Bryce decided to end the morning with a property maintenance check at Edwin Hulbert's place before going home for lunch. Edwin was a good guy outside of his issue of storing non-licensed, non-working vehicles on his large city lot in the middle of a haughty subdivision that had grown up around his old homestead.

Bryce was sure every car the old guy ever purchased was still on his property, including a gray, 1958, two door Rambler. Out of the nine vehicles parked there, that old, heavy hunk of metal was the least rusty. *They don't make cars like that anymore.* He would love to get his hands on the classic car, but Edwin wouldn't part with it when Bryce made his offer. Sadly, before too long, it was likely the man would be forced to part with all his treasures at the order of the judge unless he found a different place to store them.

He felt sorry for the old guy. His property was once country land, but the city eventually sprawled out to him, and now he had neighbors to deal with—neighbors with nice homes who didn't appreciate Edwin's treasures as much as he did.

"She's a beauty, that one," the old man said as he hobbled down the front porch steps to where Bryce stood admiring the Rambler.

Old Hulbert, as some called him, was pushing eighty and stood about 5'9" or so but it was hard to tell for sure because he walked hunched over.

Physically, he looked frail, but his mind was sharp as a tack.

"My offer still stands, if ever you want to part with her," he replied as he eyed up the vintage vehicle.

The man grinned. "I'll never part with old Betty Lou. She was my first love." He paused and flashed him a wink. "And you know how that is."

They shared a chuckle.

The nice guy Edwin was made it difficult for him to deliver today's news. Bryce tightened his grip on the clipboard he carried. If the man didn't find a suitable home for his car collection within the next thirty days, the city would do it for him, and that meant they'd wind up at the salvage yard.

Though he'd been talking with him for almost a year now, he was sure the old man would feel shocked by the news today, and then again in thirty days when the salvage yard truck arrived.

Just like clockwork, Edwin began his vehicle history spiel, but he didn't mind. He loved how passionate the old guy was about his treasures.

The hunched over man slowly lifted his skinny arm and pointed at the old Rambler. "Did I ever tell you about when I bought that beauty?" Without waiting for a reply he continued. "I swear, the second I got my own wheels the young ladies looked at me differently. No problem getting a date with that beauty in the driveway." The feisty old man elbowed him. A little glint flashed in his eyes. "No problem getting them in that big backseat either."

Bryce's heart ratcheted up a notch at the thought of Markie in the back seat of that old Rambler with him. Her under him. The two of them steaming up the windows, making out like a couple of teenagers in heat. When Edwin talked about his love for that car, Bryce easily saw himself in the back seat with that beautiful redhead who infiltrated his dreams. He'd bet his last paycheck that woman was a wild one in the sack. Not at all the conservative person she hid beneath her investigator profile at work.

Edwin pointed at the next car in line, a 1968 Dodge Charger. Truth be told, he could see himself in that vehicle, too, but that one looked like it needed a lot of work as compared to the Rambler which really intrigued him.

The old guy smiled and shook his head. "That was my racer, good old Sally Ann. She was a speedster. We would drag race on the airport runway. Cops would come, but they never caught me and Sally Ann." He winked again. "But they almost caught me and Carol Burk steaming up the windows once."

Bryce loved how the guy named his vehicles and associated each one with his love interest at the time. With as much as Edwin talked about the loves of his life, he was surprised when he found out the man never married. Maybe the ladies just couldn't compete with the cars.

After he made it through his usual stories about each vehicle, ending with the current 2008 truck sitting in his driveway, Bryce resolved himself to the fact he needed to give the poor guy the bad news about his treasures.

He pulled in a deep breath and studied the clipboard in his hand, then he lifted his gaze to meet the nice old man's.

"Edwin, you know why I'm here. And you know I appreciate how you feel about these vehicles. I understand. If I had a collection like this, I'd want to see it every day, too. But the city ordinance doesn't allow for you to keep these inoperable, unlicensed vehicles parked on your property."

"But it's *my* damn property! Who are they to tell me what I can and can't do with *my* property?" The angry man's voice echoed and he shook his hands feverishly in the air like he did every time he got overly excited. Exactly the same reaction as the last time they got to this point in their recurring conversation.

Bryce stepped back to avoid the excited man's flailing hands. He didn't think the older gentleman would ever hit him on purpose, but he wanted to keep his distance just to be safe. "I know. It doesn't seem fair."

"That's right, it's not fair!"

"What about some of the options we discussed in the past? Have you looked for any place else to store them?" Bryce asked.

Hulbert's gaze dropped to his feet. "No. I don't want to. I like seeing them every day."

The man's voice cracked, and Bryce's heart sank. This nice old guy truly loved these vehicles.

Edwin looked up. "Fine, I'll just license them then. And then my neighbors can just shut up."

"We talked about this before, remember? Even if you license them, they have to be operable, too. And you've told me none of them actually run anymore."

The man turned his head and ran his gaze back and forth over the line of vehicles as he rubbed over his chin with his fingers. Then he dropped his arms to his sides, and his shoulders slumped even more than usual.

Slowly, he turned to face Bryce. "Can you get me an extension?" A defeated look consumed his wrinkled face.

Now it was his turn to stare at his feet knowing he'd likely not be able to fulfill that request as he'd already done twice.

He returned his gaze to meet the old man's pleading eyes. "I'm sorry. This is it. Thirty days is all you have. They need to be out of sight."

Tears swelled in Hulbert's eyes.

God, how he hated this part of his job. It made him feel like the prick Markie Pearson pegged him to be.

Markie.

Why in the hell did he care what she thought of him? And why did she enter his thoughts now—again, like she did when Edwin talked about Betty Lou, the Rambler, his first love.

Bryce's phone buzzed in the holder on his hip. He yanked it from its case and cringed as he realized it was Tiana Bennett's number on the screen. He wished that psychotic woman would stop calling him. Three dates and she thought she owned him. Technically, they weren't even real dates. It wasn't like he'd actually picked her up and took her out—they'd met up, drove themselves. She was the classic example of a clinger. He couldn't imagine how clingy she'd be if they'd actually slept together.

He let the call go to voicemail and put the phone back in its holder before returning his gaze to the old man as he stared out over his cars. He reached out and touched the old man's arm. "Do you understand? I'm sorry, but thirty days is all you've got," Bryce said as he reluctantly pulled the final notice from the clipboard and handed it to him.

The man nodded slowly.

Bryce slid back into his city-issued vehicle and headed home for lunch. An eerie chill raked through him at the sight of Tiana leaning against her car in his driveway. Note to self—*No more lunching at home.* She knew his routine.

The thought crossed his mind to just drive by, but he decided against it because she'd probably just follow him back to City Hall anyhow, and he'd still have to talk with her. He parked next to the model-thin woman and slid out as slowly as possible to prolong the inevitable.

"Tiana."

She smiled and planted her sky-blue gaze on him. "Hi, Bryce. I know you're busy, which is probably why you haven't returned my calls. So, I thought I'd stop here to visit you during your lunch hour."

Great.

"Yeah, I've been busy, especially at work. Unfortunately, I only have a few minutes today, so I have to eat and run."

Her eyebrows pulled together and her full, bright red lips tipped down at the corners. "Oh, shoot. I should have stopped yesterday like I'd planned."

"Yesterday wasn't any better, and tomorrow doesn't look good either," he said, hoping she'd get the hint and not stop by, ever.

Tiana tilted her head to the side and studied him skeptically. "Hmm, you were home for almost an hour yesterday."

Unease coiled in the pit of his stomach. He'd suspected she stalked him, but now she'd just solidified his assumption. He needed to get some distance between them.

"Was I? It didn't seem like it. At any rate, I only have a minute today so I need to eat and run."

She nervously rubbed her hands together. "I brought my lunch. I'll join you."

His stomach swirled with dread. He needed to get rid of her, and not for just today but forever. Time to be firm and clear. "Look, you're a great person, but you and me, it's just not going to happen."

The woman's eyes narrowed and darkened to almost black. Her head ticked, her nostrils flared, and she moved toward him. He stepped back.

"Friends then?" she ground out between gritted teeth.

"No," he replied, knowing if he'd said yes that would ensure she'd keep coming around.

"It's that bitch in the Police Department, isn't it?"

Her accusing shrill caused anxiety to churn in the pit of his stomach. Was she talking about Markie? She was the only female who came to mind. *I need to play this smooth.*

He arched a quizzical brow. "What? Who are you talking about?"

Tiana planted her hands on her hips. "Are you kidding me? Markie. That's who. I see the way you two look at each other. You're dumping me for her. That boring, plain Jane. What the hell?"

When had she ever seen him and Markie together? They didn't hang out with each other at all...meaning Tiana was stalking him at work. It had to be. He and Markie only ever communicated at work over the property maintenance issues.

He needed to get away from this crazy lady, and now.

Intentionally, he glanced at his watch. "Well, there goes my lunch. I need to get back to work."

"Don't you dare leave me now! We're not done talking about this?"

"We're done, Tiana. Don't come back here, and don't call me anymore. Understand?"

She lunged toward him, lifting her hand in the air. He ducked her swing then spun and headed for his vehicle. The crazy stalker pounded her fist on the hood as he pulled away.

Through his rearview mirror, he watched the furious woman scramble to her car and tear out of his driveway. Was she going to follow him back to work? He hoped not. Two blocks later, she flipped on her blinker and turned off. He blew out a sigh of relief.

Why in the heck did she bring up Markie? Why not Lori? The woman he'd actually hung around with sometimes. And Tiana knew about her as they'd crossed paths while at the brewpub recently. He and Lori weren't out on a date, but out as friends. He could see how someone could mistake him and her as having a romantic relationship. Yet, her name didn't come up just now.

Bryce slipped into his office and yanked a granola bar from his desk drawer. It certainly wouldn't fill him up, but it would take the edge off.

Now, what to do about Tiana. If he went across the hall to the Police Department and reported her as a stalker, he'd be the laughing stock of City Hall. *Big*

Bad Ex-girlfriend stalks wimpy City Planner and Zoning/Property Maintenance Administrator.

Yeah, he would become a joke all right. The crazy lady weighed one hundred and ten pounds soaking wet, yet she scared the crap out of him. Still, what if she came into City Hall and raised hell? He wouldn't put it past her. The Police Department should be prepared.

He tossed the granola wrapper into the wastebasket and rose from his chair for the walk of indignity across the lobby. He made it as far as the reception desk on that side of the building before he saw Markie through the glass barrier. He did an about-face hoping she wouldn't see him. There was no way he could let *her* know he feared a tiny woman.

Glancing over his shoulder, he caught Markie's gaze. He quickly averted his and continued on his way only to have Tiana's shrill voice call out his name.

Bryce halted dead in his tracks and drew in a deep breath before turning to face her.

The crazy lady's bright, sky-blue eyes sparkled. Her soft smile stretched. "I think we just had a misunderstanding earlier. I apologize for that and hope we can get past it." The woman's voice was sweet as honey, unlike earlier in his driveway.

How was she able to pour on the charm so quickly after as angry as she'd been twenty minutes ago?

Good Lord—it was like she was a classic abuser. Abuse. Apologize. Repeat.

* * *

Through the protective glass, Markie watched Bryce as he spoke with Tiana Bennett in the lobby of City Hall. The lady was bat-shit crazy. She was in their system—had garnered some restraining orders against her in the past, even from some family members. Go figure, the womanizing city planner was involved with someone like her.

The woman looked to be quickly transitioning from happy to angry. Her voice grew louder with each passing moment. She took a step toward Bryce. He stepped back. She took another step forward and he again stepped back, but this time, he lifted his hands into the air in a submissive manner.

This isn't going well.

She bolted out of the Police Department and into the City Hall lobby just as the blonde bombshell's arm swung back.

"Tiana," Markie called out.

The woman froze in place, then turned her head to look at her.

"Is there a problem here?" Markie asked.

Tiana pulled in her outstretched arm to her head and tucked her hair behind her ear as if that was what she planned to do all along, rather than slap Bryce. Her tense facial muscles softened, and she lowered her arm.

"No problem. Just talking to Bryce."

Interestingly, the woman's tone was normal, as if she hadn't been in a total irate state moments earlier.

Markie glanced at Bryce who looked like he'd rather be anywhere but where he was at the moment. Embarrassment, shame, and relief passed through his gaze.

"Everything okay here, Bryce?" she asked.

"Yeah, no worries." He fixed his gaze on the crazy blonde. "Tiana was just leaving."

"Great, 'cause I need to see you for a minute." Markie swung her gaze to Tiana. "Have a nice day."

The woman stared at her for a moment before she whirled around on her heel and headed for the door.

Markie cast her gaze back to Bryce. "You should keep better company."

His jaw knotted. The hint of hurt mixed in his angry glare sent a tinge of shame to sift through her veins. Drilling down, she had no reason to lash out at him. He'd never done anything to hurt her but remind her of her cheating ex-fiancé. Yet, she pushed his buttons every chance she got. Treating him like shit was akin to getting back at her ex she supposed. Not really fair if she had to admit it.

"She's not my company. Never really was. The rumor mill in this town is second to none. Don't people have better things to do with their time?" His dark gaze bore into her. "You included."

Ouch.

Bryce threw his hands in the air. "Whatever. What do you need?"

"Huh?"

"You said you needed to talk to me about something. What is it?"

"Oh, that." She didn't really have anything to talk to him about. She had just wanted to get the unstable woman away from him and out of City Hall. "Nothing, never mind."

"As long as you're here. Did you get a preliminary report on Sister Ann yet?" he asked. At her silence, he continued. "Well?"

His persistence flustered her. Or, maybe it was because she still dwelled on judging him in regard to the company he kept. Truthfully, it was none of her business.

"Sorry, we haven't heard anything yet."

"All right. Well, I have work to do," Bryce said and then spun away from her.

Adrenaline pumped through her veins. She didn't want him to leave angry. "Bryce," she called out.

He looked at her over his shoulder.

"Sorry about the accusation."

His glare intensified. "Which one. The one where I killed Sister Ann or the one about me sleeping with every Tiana, Teri, and Tammy?"

He held onto his anger and didn't let her off the hook. She lowered her gaze to the tile floor. "Both."

Bryce shrugged as if her apology meant nothing to him, then he disappeared through the door to his department. Heading to his office she presumed.

The need to chase after him and make him accept her apology was overwhelming. Why did she feel like such a heel? She took two steps toward his office area before she froze in place.

Why was it important to her he accept her apology? What did it matter?

Markie sighed. She knew why, but the shards of fear that stabbed at her heart every time she looked at him kept her from admitting she liked him—really liked him.

He wasn't at all the jackass she tried to paint him to be, and the story she'd heard about him this morning proved it yet again—about his volunteer efforts at the Boys and Girls Club. He'd spent hours upon hours helping to remodel the facility at their new location, thereby, leaving his own house remodeling project at a near standstill in order to get the new building ready for the club so they could accommodate more kids. Jerks don't do that kind of stuff—put others before themselves.

But, viewing Bryce as a jerk helped her keep him at a distance, and distance was good—helped protect her heart from another heartbreak.

The thrill zipping through her body at present indicated she'd have to dig deeper—work harder to find a way to keep him in the jerk—safe zone.

Chapter Four

Bryce parked in his usual spot behind City Hall and reluctantly slid out of his vehicle. Did he dare enter the building today? It had been a tough week already, and he wasn't sure he had it in him to face another day like Monday or Tuesday. One thing was for sure, there was no way he would be doing any property maintenance checks today.

How had it come to this? He'd become the dreaded property maintenance guy. He looked down at where his real leg used to be—the reminder of how he ended up where he did. If not for the improvised explosive device that nearly took his life, he'd probably either still be in the Marine Corps or a police officer, utilizing the Police Science degree he'd earned before joining the service. But no, without a leg, being a soldier or a police officer were no longer options.

Lucky me. I got to become the property maintenance guy.

A small part of him held hope, since he obtained a Public Administration degree after returning home, he'd get promoted, or find an administrator position, something more than being a planning/zoning assistant and the property maintenance guy.

Bryce sighed as he entered his office and flipped through some design sketches for a new apartment complex being proposed to the city by a well-established developer. Though it should be a slam dunk by the planning commission next week, he still had to prepare a thorough executive summary for them to review.

After completing the paperwork for the meeting agenda, he slipped into the records room to work on digitizing the property record files, a job he'd decided to take on several months back. It would probably take him a year to finish the low priority project, but he didn't mind working on it a little at a time when he desired some mindless, yet needed, work.

As he scanned documents, his mind drifted to his encounters with Tiana. Not just her though, but the others like her as well. On one hand, surrounding himself with women like her, selfish, uncaring women with whom he knew he'd have no future, shielded him from having to deal with his intimacy issues. If his father's marriage record wasn't already bad enough, he had to add his inadequate body to boot.

It had been five years since he lost his leg just below his knee and damaged his genitals, and in all that time he still hadn't attempted intercourse. Sweat ran down his sides. Fearing what a woman would think at the sight of his inadequate, incomplete body, he avoided intimacy, yet he fiercely longed for it. He was lonely, both physically and mentally. Anxiety ripped through him. What scared him even more was the possibility he wouldn't be able to father children, or worse yet, perform.

Even with all the months he'd spent in rehab and therapy after he'd lost his leg, he still couldn't shake the mental incompleteness he felt. Many soldiers had been injured in a far greater capacity than he and they seemed to be able to work through their issues, but he still felt like he was on square one, and in his mind, square two looked to be such a leap he didn't think he'd ever make it.

Markie Pearson's lovely, freckled face flashed in his mind. His chest hollowed knowing he'd never be able to get and keep a spirited woman like her. She'd need a complete man. A man who could surely satisfy her. His chest hollowed. It was hopeless.

He swallowed hard, just as his stomach growled, jolting him back into reality. A quick glance at his watch let him know it was time for lunch. Fearing Tiana would stop at his house during his lunch hour, he'd chosen to pack his lunch today and just eat at his desk in solitude.

Back in his office, he began to unwrap his sandwich when someone knocked on his door. He squeezed his eyes shut. *Please God, not Tiana.*

When he lifted his lids and turned his head he found Lori Holloway peeking through the narrow glass on his door. *Thank God.* He motioned his bar league dart partner in.

They'd met when he first moved to town and quickly became friends. Though he knew she wanted more from him, she was shy and never really pushed the issue after her first attempt when he'd let her down easy. He just didn't feel the same.

She sat in the chair opposite his desk and flipped her long brown hair over her shoulder. "I hear you had a rough couple of days."

One thing he learned promptly when moving to this small town was that everybody knew everyone's business. It was a wonder he was able to hide the truth about his leg. At least he'd thought he was successful. Nobody talked about it.

"You could say that."

She nodded sympathetically.

Bryce pointed at his lunch sprawled out on his desk. "Did you eat yet? I've plenty if you want some."

Lori smiled warmly. "I already ate. I just wanted to check in on you to see how you were doing."

She really was a nice, caring woman. Just not his type. Why nobody'd scooped her up yet was beyond him.

"All's good."

"Has there been any scuttlebutt about who killed Sister Ann?" she asked.

"Not that I've heard. But for a moment there, I think Investigator Pearson thought it was me."

Adrenaline shot through his veins at the thought he was actually a person of interest.

Lori arched a brow. "Really?"

He shrugged. "I get it, seeing it was me who found her, but still. I've worked here for a couple of years now. You'd think they'd know me by now."

Lori shook her head as her dark brown gaze held his. "I know. But you know, every time something like this happens and they interview family and friends of the guilty party on television, they always say, '*He was the nicest guy. I can't believe he'd do something like this. He was the best neighbor.*' You know, that kind of stuff."

His chest tightened. She was right. It was only logical the police—Markie consider him a suspect, but it still hurt.

"I suppose. Plus, it doesn't help these property maintenance issues are nothing but a thorn in my side, and I've complained about them in the past to Markie during the ones we had to work on together."

"Yeah. I recall how you feel about them, and from what you've said, I don't blame you for complaining. It sounds justified."

His kind friend's comment was true. His grievances were warranted but now they made him look guilty.

"I know, but now I wish I hadn't said anything."

"Do you want to get a drink after work? Take your mind off things?"

He thought for a moment. With as good as that sounded a quiet night home alone sounded better. "Raincheck?"

Disappointment flashed in her gaze. "Sure."

The door banged open. The scent of coconut infiltrated his nostrils. He knew it was Markie even before his head snapped in that direction.

Her reproachful glare pinned him in place and held for a moment before she swung it to Lori. The meek woman shifted awkwardly in her chair and looked to be purposely avoiding Markie's glower.

Markie moved her gaze back to him. "We need to talk." Her stern voice sent a chill up his spine.

Lori sprang out of her chair. "I was just leaving."

Markie stood rigid in front of his desk. She looked flustered. Unusual for her.

"Did you hear the latest?" she asked.

He was almost too afraid to ask. "Latest what?"

"Where were you this morning at about eleven a.m.?"

"Here."

"You weren't in your office when I checked a while ago, and nobody seemed to know where you were."

The chill in his spine spread to the rest of his nerve endings. "What's going on?"

"First, tell me where you were."

"I was in the records room digitizing documents." Feeling defensive, he turned toward his computer, called up the files, and pointed at his screen. "See, look. You can see the time stamp on these, proving I was in the records room scanning documents."

Markie leaned over his shoulder. Her enticing coconut scent penetrated his nostrils, playing sweet havoc on his senses even though she grilled him.

"How do I know Colleen or Mary didn't create those files?"

Though he knew he could prove his innocence, the frustration in his body caused his muscles to constrict. "Well, why don't you just go ask them if you don't believe me?" he said as he shook his head in quick, sharp movements while he lifted his hand and gestured toward the door. His tone had been prickly by design.

Markie let out a minty breath. Her accusing, taut facial muscles loosened into a repentant look of understanding.

What in the hell is going on?

She moved away from him, stepped around his desk, and took a seat in the chair on the opposite side.

"The fire department was called to a vehicle fire today at Old Hulbert's place."

He sprang forward in his chair. "Is he okay?"

She shook her head. "I'm afraid not. He was in the vehicle."

His body quivered. He swallowed hard. "Is he dead?" he asked, knowing the answer already.

Markie nodded.

Poor Edwin. He really liked the old guy.

"What happened?"

"We're still trying to figure that out. But the empty gas can lying on its side next to the vehicle leads me to believe it was not an accident. The fire marshal is investigating as we speak."

An array of emotions collided through him—sympathy, grief, fear, apprehension. Two of his code violators in one week? The property maintenance ones in particular? Was someone targeting them? These poor people didn't intentionally cause anyone harm. So they were hoarders—junk collectors. That didn't mean they were bad or vindictive people. In fact, when it came to Edwin and Sister Ann, they pretty much stuck to themselves.

Admittedly, this didn't look good for him. Hence, why Markie was in his office staring at him as if he should have some sort of explanation for her. But he didn't. He hadn't a clue why this was happening.

"Which vehicle?" As soon as he asked the question, he wished he could take it back. What did it matter?

Markie tilted her head to the side. Her long, red ponytail flopped. God he loved her sexy red hair. His fingers itched to reach out and comb through those silky looking strands.

"His truck. Go figure, none of the beaters."

Her use of the word beaters made him sad. To Edwin, those were treasures.

"Does anyone else have access to your computer passwords?"

So, this was how it would be, she was going to continue to interrogate him. Even after that look of belief she'd flashed him moments ago.

"No. It was me in the records room creating those files. Nobody else."

"When was the last time you saw Old Hulbert?"

Reaching back, he grabbed the clipboard off the credenza behind him, then he placed it on his desk facing the accusing investigator. He pointed at the date and timeline on the report attached to the clipboard. "Yesterday. I was at his house following up on his property maintenance issue. I was there from ten-thirty to just before noon."

"Why so long? It wasn't hard to see that he hadn't made one bit of effort to remove those rust buckets from his property."

"They're not rust buckets," he snapped back. The quizzical look on her face had him wanting to explain further. "To you, they may be crappy old cars—junk, but to him, they were prize possessions—a valuable collection. He had a history with them—fond memories associated with each and every one."

Adrenaline rushed his veins as he spoke, sending the pitch of his voice higher than normal. Why couldn't people have just left the nice old man alone?

Markie leaned forward. He thought she was just going to look more closely at the report, but instead, she placed her soft hand over his. That beautiful, bright emerald gaze of hers locked onto his.

"I'm sorry for your loss."

His heart slammed against his ribcage. Her touch was too dangerous. He wanted to pull away but couldn't. It led to him wanting more from her. This was exactly why he avoided her—kept his distance.

He knew he wouldn't have the strength to fend her off once he endured the feel of her.

Losing himself in her emerald gaze was hard enough when he wasn't able to avoid it. But her touch right now proved he'd been right all along. She had his senses begging for more, starting with a kiss to those full red lips of hers, and ending with...

Bryce closed his thoughts off and yanked his hand away from hers. He couldn't think about that. He just couldn't. It could never happen. Sheer defeat encompassed every cell in his body. He had the needs of every normal man, but he wasn't normal—he was incomplete.

Her wide-eyed, shocked gaze transitioning to pity made him feel even worse.

Markie's heart cracked in half. Oddly though, not because of his rejection of her sincere gesture, but for him, for whatever it was that had bruised him so badly he couldn't accept her heartfelt compassion.

The compassion in his eyes when he defended Old Hulbert told the story of their friendship, and she honestly felt sympathy for him for his loss. Womanizer or not, this man cared for the old guy. She'd taken enough psychology classes to earn her Master's degree in Police Science to recognize Bryce had endured something horrific in his life to cause him to behave the way he did toward women. What it was, she didn't know, but the need to find out—fix it, was overwhelming.

She'd have to do a bit of research on Bryce. Get his story. She studied him as he stared out the window, off in his own little world. The man was elusive, and since she didn't do his background check when he was hired, she actually knew very little about him except for the fact he was a casanova. He looked and acted like a player and hanging around with Tiana Bennett only solidified that. That woman liked the smooth ones.

Thinking back, she recalled hearing recently that Bryce had been in the Marine Corps—did a tour in Afghanistan. But that was all she knew, and it should have nothing to do with why he went through women like they were disposable.

When he returned his gaze to her, those dark eyes of his had transitioned from caring and grieving to cold and off-putting. Classic *I'm going to push you away now* eyes. Too late though, she'd seen it. There was more to this man than what he let the general population see. He was kind and caring. Was his womanizing attitude his way of pushing people away—keeping them at a safe distance? But why? What made him do that? Self-esteem issues?

She was dying to find out why this man who seemed to have everything going for him possibly lacked the self-esteem to let people past the wall of defense he'd constructed around him.

Markie leaned back in her seat. "I'm sorry. You're right. Those cars were important to Old Hulbert, I shouldn't have been so cold about it."

He shrugged as if it didn't matter, as if he didn't care what the old man thought of the vehicles. Unlike a minute ago when he would have defended Edwin's actions to his death. Yep, she'd lost him in those couple minutes.

"Whatever. It's not my deal. Now it can get cleaned up and the neighbors will be happy. Maybe you should question them. They all had something to gain by getting Edwin out of the way."

"I will be."

"Did you have any more questions for me or can I eat my lunch now?" he asked. His tone oozed with annoyance as he grabbed his sandwich and took a bite.

Markie gripped the arms of the chair and pushed herself up. "No, not for now. I'll see you later."

He stopped chewing and swallowed. A muscle in his jaw bulged and twitched. "Looking forward to it."

His lie filled the room, pushing her through the door.

On her way back to her office, she stopped by Captain Tomie's office. "Got a minute?"

Looking up from the mounds of paperwork on his desk, the middle-aged man's light blue gaze met her's. "What's up?"

She stepped in and took a seat. "I just talked to Bryce. He was here all morning...during the car explosion at old Hulbert's."

He nodded, and she shifted in her chair.

"Something else on your mind?" he asked.

Why wouldn't he ask her that? He was a trained observer, and she probably looked nervous—antsy.

"I'm just curious about his story?"

The man's blue-eyed gaze narrowed. "Who's story? Edwin's?"

"No, not Old Hulbert's. I've known him my whole life. He was just an old bachelor, a kind old soul who minded his own business. He and my grandfather were actually buddies. Both served in Korea."

The captain's thick eyebrows pulled together, and he tilted his head to the side. "So then, Bryce?"

Her cheeks heated. She knew she needed to tread carefully or he'd figure her out.

"Yes, Bryce. When I talked to him just now about Edwin he was...well, at first he seemed sad, like he grieved his death, but then as the conversation continued, he turned cold and hard as stone. He went from one extreme to the other in a matter of seconds."

He nodded. "Hmm."

She stared at him, hoping for more of a response.

"He was in the military...Marines. Been out a few years. I know he saw some action in Afghanistan. Maybe he's still working through some shit."

"But to transition so quickly from one end of the spectrum to the other seems...distressing."

Captain Tomie leaned back in his chair, crossed his arms over his chest, and mulled it over with a look of understanding on his face. She wondered if the mention of the military, Korea and Afghanistan, had him thinking about his own days when he served in Desert Shield and Desert Storm.

He refocused on her. "That behavior is not all uncommon for a soldier. On the battlefield, it's necessary to suppress...control emotions in order to make critical decisions...life-saving decisions. It becomes a way of life, so when returning home it's hard to shut off. It can take some time to work through that. Unfortunately, some veterans never do."

"I wonder if..."

Captain raised his hand cutting off her words. "Don't. Leave him be. I recognize that *I want to fix it—him*, look on your face. I've seen it first hand on my wife, my mother, and even my sisters."

VALERIE J. CLARIZIO

"But…"

His hand went up again.

Her cheeks heated. He knew how she felt about Bryce.

"I understand. Everyone just wants to help. But having been a person who's been there…"

The man paused, lost in familiar memories, she supposed.

He refocused. "Tell you what, I'll have a chat with him, see where it leads."

That was her cue. Leave it to the veterans. "Thank you, sir."

Still, she wanted to help the man she'd vowed to stay away from. What on earth was wrong with her? She should take the opportunity to run as far away from him as possible. Hurting, wounded, or not, a man like Bryce was bad for her because whether or not he had a good excuse for being a womanizer, he still was one.

Chapter Five

Bryce held up the sheet of drywall as his dad screwed it in place, making it a lot easier than when working alone. After the news of Edwin's death, all he'd wanted to do after his shift was go home and work on his house. Restoring the old, two-story, brick home relaxed him—allowed him to grind off his frustrations in solitude, but when his father offered to drive up and help for the evening, he took him up on the offer, hoping to make some noticeable progress.

"It's really starting to shape up," his dad commented.

"Yeah, slow but sure."

"You'll get there."

Bryce pulled another sheet of drywall from the pile and held it in place. It was coming along, and he couldn't be more proud that his own two hands were pulling it together.

"I've heard about those murders this week on the news. Odd," His dad commented.

"Yes, it is strange," he agreed. Anxiety swirled in his gut at the thought of the late Sister Ann and Edwin Hulbert, and the fact he'd been questioned about the murders.

"Do the police have any idea who's behind them?"

Bile rose in his throat. "Me." There, he'd said it. Out loud.

His father froze in place. The noise of the cordless screwdriver stopped. His head snapped in Bryce's direction. Shock laced his dad's gaze. "What did you say?"

"They've questioned me."

"Are you kidding me?" His dad set the screwdriver down and faced him directly. At least his father believed he didn't do it. He had some support.

"No, I'm not. They really did." Sweat beaded on his brow at the recollection of Markie's accusation.

"Why did they question you?"

"Well, both the victims are property maintenance code violators."

"What does that mean?"

"They're people I've cited and am currently working with to clean up their properties."

"So the victims had reason to dislike you?"

"Yes."

His dad pulled a frown. "So if they didn't like you wouldn't it be the other way around?"

"You mean they'd want to kill me, instead of me killing them?" Bryce's throat squeezed around those words. His father had a good point, but he didn't like the thought someone would want to kill him any better than him being accused of murder.

"That would make more sense," his dad stated with a nod.

"I know, right?"

"Well, shit. Now what?" his dad asked as he raked his hand over his face.

"I don't know. And that damn Investigator Pearson is on my ass about it."

"The gorgeous redhead?"

"That's the one. Don't let her cute," Bryce bent over and grabbed another sheet of drywall off the stack, "little," he spun and stepped toward where it needed to be hung, "innocent," he placed it to the wall and glanced over his shoulder at his dad, "look she

42

portrays all the time deceive you. She's a pain in the ass and tough as nails."

His father studied him as he stepped toward him. The corners of his mouth tilted up. "So, you like her?"

Heat flooded his face. He'd said too much. The one person in this world who could read him like a book was his dad, yet he still ran off at the mouth. Thinking back, he hadn't said too much about Markie, but it was enough for his dad to know, or perhaps it was his tone. Who knew for sure?

"No. I'm just telling you like it is."

"Uh huh. Sure." Now his dad's eyes were even smiling.

"It's not like that."

"If you tell me you don't care for her in that way I'll believe you." He paused, looked out the window, and then returned his gaze to him, his face sober as a judge. "You know, it's okay to put yourself out there when the good ones come along. You're judging yourself harder than the right woman will."

Bryce averted his gaze. He didn't want to have this awful conversation again, though it had been a while since the topic had come up.

"Son?"

His father's caring but solemn tone drew his attention.

"Don't automatically shut the door on potential happiness. Go out on a limb and take a chance now and then. When you find the right one, it will be worth it."

A quiver raked through his body. Easy for him to say, his dad didn't have a clue as to what he was going through or how he felt when it came to women—sex—his fear of lack of performance due to his injuries…

This subject made him want to crawl out of his skin. Why couldn't they just hang the drywall like planned? Why did they have to talk at all? And what in the hell did his father know about love? The guy was on his fifth marriage, and this time his step-mother was only thirty-two years old—two years older than Bryce.

Bryce set down the sheet of drywall he held, fixed his gaze on his father, and cocked his head to the side.

"Worth it? The right one? Like you know how to pick them. You're on your fifth right one."

A tinge of anger and disappointment laced his father's dark eyes, and Bryce knew the displeasure in his dad's gaze wasn't channeled in his own direction, but it was dissatisfaction in him for his cold comments. Immediately, he regretted his words.

His father leaned back on his heels and crossed his arms over his chest. "You know, son, I view it a little differently than you. I thank God every day I was lucky enough to find love five times. Not many people are that lucky, and if you don't change your attitude, you won't find it once. And it's a mighty good feeling to pass on just because you're afraid of—"

Bryce lifted his hand. "Just stop already! I'm done with this conversation, and I don't want to have it again. You can't tell me being divorced four times is lucky. It's ludicrous—absolutely stupid to think so."

The older man's facial muscles tensed.

Shame filled every cell of Bryce's body. Again, like so many other times in the past, he resorted to meanness to cut people out of his life. It was easier that way. Push them away so he could keep from admitting the truth about his intimacy issues. Even if it meant isolating himself from the closest people to him.

Bryce sighed, why he tried to keep his self-esteem and intimacy issues from his father was beyond him since the man already knew.

"Well, I think we're done for the night. I know I've had enough," his dad said flatly as he unfolded his arms, then spun to leave.

He knew he should call out after him and apologize, but stubbornness closed his throat.

His father opened the squeaky, worn wooden door, paused, and looked over his shoulder. "Bryce, let me remind you that you lost your leg and left nut in Afghanistan, not your heart. I'm not sure where you lost that along the way, but you're going to die a lonely man if you don't find it and open it up again. There are a lot of people who love you, and I can guarantee there will be more in the future if you let them. Despite your hurtful comments a few moments ago, know my door is always open to you, and I'll do whatever I can to help you through."

Bryce managed a nod before his dad stepped through the doorway. He felt like an absolute heel. Grade A prick.

Chapter Six

Bryce glanced at the clock, 4:30 p.m., finally. This had to be the longest workweek ever. At least Thursday and Friday, unlike the first three days of the week, were uneventful. No more dead bodies had to be a good sign.

Unfortunately though, there'd been no progress on catching the killer. At least as far as he knew. And with Markie popping into his office a couple of times a day, he'd surely know if she was making headway. What he didn't understand, however, was why she wore that sympathetic look all the time. Yes, she'd figured out he grieved Edwin's death, but it wasn't like they'd been best buds or anything. After further thought, her look bordered on pity more than sympathy. It was the same stupid look people gave him when they'd noticed he was missing a leg. God, he hated that pathetic look.

The pity look she'd flashed him, the one that seemed to bore deep into his soul, had him wondering if she somehow found out about his military background and injuries. He did his best not to talk about either with anyone. And the fact he never wore shorts helped hide his prosthetic leg. Wishing he could wear shorts, he'd bought some and put them on, but every time he reached his front door his shaky hands wouldn't turn the knob.

Part of him wondered if Markie was the reason behind the unusual mid-day visit from Captain Tomie. The busy man rarely roamed the building, let alone popped into his office for no particular reason. Sure, they discussed property maintenance issues sometimes, but that topic hadn't come up during this particular conversation. Tomie used the prior week's Fourth of July holiday as a transition into a conversation about their military service. The very fireworks poor Sister Ann probably missed because she'd been stuffed inside a freezer.

Like his dad, the man sitting opposite his desk served in Desert Shield and Desert Storm. Both veterans escaped physical injury, but unlike Tomie, his father suffered from Gulf War Syndrome. Or if Tomie did, he didn't let on.

Bryce propped his elbows up on his desk, closed his eyes, and rested his head in his hands. The look of understanding on Tomie's face and the man's final words as he exited the office ran through his mind.

"Son, if ever you need to talk, about anything, know I'm here, and only across the hall. No one needs to fight—cope—alone."

The former soldier knew. Bryce swallowed hard. Did Markie? She was the last person he wanted to know about the demons that haunted him. She was the one person he secretly wished thought of him as strong—whole.

Lifting his head, he yanked his cell phone from his pocket and tapped in his dad's number.

"Hello:"

"Hey, Dad."

"Something wrong?"

He drew in a long breath and let it out.

"Bryce, are you okay?"

"Yes. I just wanted to call and apologize for the other day...for being such a jackass. I know you're only trying to help, and I appreciate that. And as for my comment about your marriages, it was uncalled for. I'm sorry. I am glad you are happy."

"No worries. Hey, your brother will be on leave in a couple of weeks and he's coming home for a few days. Why don't you take some time off and we'll go fishing or something. Just us guys, like in the old days. I'm sure your brother will want to see you."

Bryce blew out a mental sigh. Carter. He loved his younger brother but seeing him only added to his pain. Carter was the perfect Marine. Exactly who he thought he'd be. Climbing the ranks—whole.

Everything he wasn't now.

"And just so you know, he's bringing a girl home to meet us. Seeing as he's never brought anyone home before, I'm guessing this Lindsey's probably the one. I saw her picture on the internet. She's beautiful."

Of course she is. Carter would have it all. A decorated military career, beautiful wife, a son who follows in his steps, and a daughter who becomes a CEO or something. Probably even a champion show dog, too. Meanwhile, he would get to continue irritating everyone as the dreaded property maintenance guy.

Life is great.

"Bryce?"

"Yeah."

"Please promise me you'll come to see your brother when he's home. He loves you. We all love you."

A lump rose in his throat. He loved them, too, but seeing Carter was hard. So unbelievably hard.

He choked down the obstruction blocking his voice. "I'll be there. Text me the dates, and I'll set up a fishing charter for us here."

"You got it. Say, do you want some help with the house next week at all? I'd help this weekend but Bridget's company picnic is tomorrow."

"Yeah, maybe Wednesday or Thursday night. We'll touch base later about that."

"Sounds good. Bye."

"Okay, bye."

Bryce stuffed his phone in his pocket, logged off his computer, and flipped off his office lights. When he stepped into the lobby, he was surprised to find a handful of management staff there, Markie included. On a typical Friday afternoon staff practically ran out of the building at closing time.

"Hey, Bryce. We were just trying to decide where to go for appetizers and a beer. Wanna join us?" Administrator Clayton Johnston asked.

All he wanted to do was go home, lock himself in the house, have a couple of beers, and not think about the week he'd had, but Markie's emerald gaze had him suggesting they go to O'Malley's Pub for some Irish nachos.

O'Malley's was a good choice for a couple of reasons. Number one, he'd hear Markie talk about how much she liked the place, and number two, Tiana used to date the owner's son and refused to step foot in the bar after he dumped her. At least he could end this awful week without having to see her out. He hadn't seen her since she made a scene in the city hall lobby on Tuesday, and he ignored her handful of calls since then. Going to O'Malley's *should* ensure he wouldn't have to see her while enjoying some drinks.

"How does that work for everyone?" Clayton asked.

They all nodded.

Cautioning on the side of safety, Bryce decided to ditch his SUV at home and walk back downtown to the bar. Though he was almost positive Tiana would not go into O'Malley's, the last thing he needed was to chance her coming in because she saw his vehicle parked there. Additionally, after the rough week he'd had, he wasn't sure how many drinks it would take to calm his nerves. He was almost positive it would be more than the standard two, so driving would be out of the question.

In less than fifteen minutes, he stepped through the front door of the pub. The bells clinked against the glass and most heads turned in his direction. The city hall gang sat at a long table near the dart boards. He edged his way past the pool tables toward them. O'Malley's had a pretty good business, and being a Friday night it probably wouldn't take an hour yet before the place was packed.

Bryce fought the urge to grab the open seat next to Markie like his heart begged him to, and he took up residence between Clayton and Fire Chief Bosley on the opposite side of the table. Perhaps it was a mistake to sit down one person across from her. It would be too easy for his gaze to gravitate to her, and soak in those sexy emerald eyes of hers. But then, to sit next to her would have sent his sense of touch begging him for satisfaction. Yes, he was better off sitting where he'd chosen. Markie was the look but don't touch type for him. If he touched her, he'd definitely want more, and that was out of the question.

The waitress, Sarah, served up several appetizers for them to share, then asked him what he wanted to drink. He ordered a beer, then focused on the jalapeno poppers in front of the gorgeous redhead across the table.

She scooped a popper out of the basket, set it on her plate, and then lifted the basket toward him, swirling it around. Tempting him. Teasing him.

"Here you go. I know these are your favorites." Her full red lips lifted into a soft smile.

Poppers *were* his favorite. How did she know that? Well, she was a trained observer, and this wasn't the first time they'd all gone out after work.

She moved the basket closer to him, and her smile widened. A genuine smile that sent his heart racing.

He took the basket from her, set a couple of poppers on his plate, and then passed it along.

Moments later, Sarah returned and set his frosty mug in front of him along with a folded-up piece of paper. She winked, spun, and sashayed away, her full hips swinging flirtatiously. Sarah was a pretty, full-figured woman who definitely knew how to work the crowd for tips, but she'd never really hit on him in the past.

His gaze returned to the small, white piece of paper lying next to his beer. Curiosity got the best of him.

"You never have a tough time with the ladies, do you?" Clayton joked as he reached over and slapped him on his shoulder blade. "I'm jealous. Us short, chubby guys have to work a lot harder to garner the attention of the beauties," the stocky man added with a chuckle.

Instantaneously, he looked at Markie. No trace of the warm smile that had been on her face seconds ago remained. Sadly, it was replaced with a thin line. After a couple of beats, she averted her eyes.

Disappointment raked through him. Deep down, he knew Markie thought of him as a player, and though that was safer for him, he didn't like it. With each passing day, he wanted even more for her to like him—not think of him as a selfish, womanizer. But, intentionally keeping her on the other side of the barrier he built around himself, at her own choice, was safer for him and her. That way he'd never be given the opportunity to disappoint her—let her down. Yes, the timing of a note from Sarah was perfect, because that look he and Markie shared over the basket of poppers was too inviting—compelling to the point where he wanted to demolish those protective walls surrounding him.

To fortify his walls of defense, he looked at the chunky man with curious eyes sitting beside him, pulled a wicked smile, and unfolded the note from Sarah.

The weighty man grunted as he leaned over to take a peak but Bryce quickly folded the note again so he couldn't see the words scribbled out.

"Come on. You're not going to share it with us?" Clayton asked while the other men at the table chimed in wanting the scoop.

He tucked the note into his shirt pocket, disregarding the men's heckles. But he couldn't ignore the complete look of disdain on Markie's face. He should be happy, he got the exact result he wanted from her.

So why did he feel like such a heel and disheartened?

What was even more disappointing was what the note said. *I know you're with that whore you cheating asshole!*

The note certainly wasn't from Sarah.

Bryce swung his gaze around the room expecting to see Tiana perched on a stool somewhere, but he didn't. Yet, somehow she knew he sat across the table from Markie, and he already knew what she thought of her.

Later, just to be sure, he'd have to ask the waitress who gave her the paper to deliver. But for now, he'd let everyone believe what they all assumed, that it was Sarah's number or something similar. He wondered if she knew what was on the note or if she just delivered it.

* * *

Markie eyed Bryce's hand as he patted his shirt pocket where he'd placed the note from Sarah. His self-assured smile irritated her. Had every female in this town dated him at some point?

What struck her odd though was the brief look of distress that flashed through his eyes as he read the note. When he realized everyone's attention was focused on him, the look quickly transitioned to his usual overly-confident one she'd grown to despise. What did the note say to cause a concerned look, though only temporarily?

The mysteries of Bryce intrigued her more and more every day. She began to think he wanted everyone to think he was something he wasn't. His words, and larger actions sent one message, but his eyes and the small things he did sent another. His fingers patting his pocket didn't send the same message his concerned gaze sent.

Sarah delivered another round of beers, giving no special treatment to Bryce this time, and vice versa, causing Markie to want to see that note even more.

It didn't take long for the conversation to turn to the murders of Sister Ann and Edwin Hulbert. Bryce's jaw tensed and a muscle above his right eyebrow pulsed. He gripped the handle of his beer mug and took a long swig. His knuckles turned white.

Markie felt sorry for him. Not only did it look bad that two people he knew were murdered, he genuinely grieved the loss of Old Hulbert.

The non-law enforcement people at the table, other than Bryce, offered their theories about who could have committed the murders and why. She, Captain Tomie, and Chief Bosley listened attentively. Maybe their theories would spark something.

"Bryce, I'd like to hear your thoughts?" Tomie cut in.

He studied the former Marine for a few beats before the man spoke again. "I'm serious. With your background and education, I'd like to hear what you think."

His background and education? What did being a Marine and holding a degree in Public Administration have to do with investigating murders? Markie couldn't help but wonder.

The sheepish look on Bryce's face was out of the norm.

"I don't really have anything. It's just unfortunate."

"That's crap. What do you think?" Captain pushed.

Bryce leaned forward and rested his elbows on the table. "I've only lived here a couple of years so I don't know everyone like you guys do, so I have no idea if there could be a connection between the nun and Edwin. Are they related? Did they go to the same school or church?"

"We didn't find a lineage connection, and I don't know where, or if, Edwin was a church goer. The only connection we have so far is they were both prop..."

"Property maintenance issues for the city. Code violators. Subjects I was working with," Bryce finished for the captain.

Tomie nodded along with the chief and everyone else at the table.

"Yeah, that's about all we have right now," Captain replied as his gaze cut over to her. "But Markie's on it so I'm sure we'll get some answers soon."

Pride sifted through her at the conviction in the captain's tone when he spoke of her.

"I'll do my best," she replied.

"I know you will," he replied before swinging his gaze back to Bryce. "So, any thoughts?"

Markie wondered if Bryce realized his hand had drifted back to his shirt pocket where he'd stuffed the note from the waitress. Did something in that note provide a theory—suspect for Bryce? She considered point blank asking, but the tight set of his jaw, and clouded eyes indicated he would offer nothing at all, especially about the note.

"Sorry, sir, I've got nothing," Bryce said before he grabbed his mug and took another swig, draining it dry.

Sir. Of course that's what he'd call a former Marine officer.

"Well, if you think of anything let me know," Captain replied, letting Bryce off the hook.

The waitress came by and swiped Bryce's mug off the table. "Want another?"

"No. I'll take a Jack and Coke instead."

Hitting the hard stuff. Who could blame him after the week he'd had.

Bryce caught her stare. "I walked here."

"I didn't say a word," Markie replied.

"The disapproving look on your face said enough," he snapped back.

She felt Captain Tomie's gaze burning a hole in her, and she risked a glance in his direction. His hushing look silenced her.

Clayton and both the fire and police chiefs finished their beers and left. About five minutes later, Captain Tomie, Building Inspector Franke, and Assessor Lutz followed suit, leaving only her and Bryce at the table. They sat in uncomfortable silence. Markie milked her beer. She could certainly use another one, but she needed to drive so two was her limit.

"You don't need to sit here and babysit me. I'm fine," he blurted coldly. "Or, are you here to make sure I don't kill any more of my code violators?"

"I'm not babysitting you, nor are you a suspect. I'm just...I'm just having a beer with a co-worker, but if you don't become better company you will be sitting here by yourself."

"That's the way I prefer it."

"Why are you being such an asshole when I'm trying to be nice to you?"

"Nice? You think you're being nice? Sorry, but I think you need to work on your soft skills, and need to do a better job of getting control of your body language if you want to come off as a nice, concerned friend."

He was really starting to irritate her.

"When did you become a body language expert?"

"I didn't say I was, but yours is so transparent it's kind of hard to misinterpret."

Wasn't that interesting? Little did he know she was apparently a master at disguising her body language. Her heart ached for him, yet right now, he seemed to be under the impression she was judging— already sentencing him for the murders of Sister and Edwin. Or, was he reading her correctly, and this effort by him was the classic attempt to push her away—push away anyone who tried to help him?

Markie willed her tense muscles to relax as she tried to figure out a way to turn this conversation around. "My apologies. The job hardens a person. Makes us skeptical. I don't believe you had anything to do with the murders of Sister and Edwin, and I don't care how much you drink. I just wanted to come out and have a couple of drinks with some friends to help unwind after a pretty tough week."

His gaze landed on the table top. "Me, too."

After a few moments of silence, Lori Holloway flitted up to the table. "Hi, Markie. Hi Bryce. Mind if I join you?"

Actually, she did mind. Lori was nice enough, but she'd hoped to use this time to get to know Bryce better, find out more about him and why he behaved the way he did. Lori would just get in the way of that.

Bryce stood and pulled out the chair next to him for the woman to sit.

She sat and set her drink on the table. "Busy in here tonight," the woman commented as she smiled and looked adoringly at him.

Bryce returned her smile, but his gaze did not match Lori's. His was more of a friendly acknowledgment. *Hmm, so this one didn't do anything for the man. Interesting, but good.*

Markie eyed her empty glass. She should leave, but her feet felt as heavy as cinderblocks, and curiosity kept her weighted down in her chair. Maybe if Bryce had enough alcohol his tongue would loosen about his life.

"Do you want another drink?" the waitress asked as she reached down and snatched Markie's glass.

"No thanks."

The waitress nodded and hustled away.

Markie sat quietly, listening to Bryce and Lori chat about their dart league and some upcoming community events they'd planned to attend. The desperate woman threw out vibe after vibe to draw deeper attention from Bryce, but his good defense kept her at arm's length and in the dreaded friend zone. She had always wondered if he and Lori had been, or were an item, but from what she witnessed now she knew the answer.

Lori was an easy target for a player, yet Bryce wasn't taking the bait. Was he not the man she'd pegged him to be? A little thrill snapped through her. She hoped she was mistaken about him. A true player would take anyone, right?

When Bryce finished his whiskey, Lori asked if he wanted another. At his hesitation, Markie thought he'd order another, but then he shook his head. Disappointment washed over Lori's face, but she kept her friendly smile in place.

"All right, then."

Bryce stood.

Lori followed suit and fixed her admiring gaze on him. "I didn't see your vehicle in the parking lot, do you need a ride home?" The woman's tone was hopeful.

"No thanks."

Hmm, still fending her off. Or, is he clueless to her intentions. No, nobody could be that naive.

Lori stepped toward him, gave him a quick hug, then took a step back. "Okay then. See you later." She spun and left.

Markie stood and followed Bryce out the door and into the parking lot. Tiana's shrill voice screeched Bryce's name. He flinched and glanced at Markie. His gaze begging her to save him. She would bet her last paycheck he'd never say the words though.

Tiana placed her hand on Bryce's shoulder and planted her pinning glare on Markie, staking her claim.

"Just catching an after-work drink with some coworkers?" Tiana asked him. The vile woman leaned into Bryce's side. "Do you want another? I'd love to buy you one, but not here." She looked down the alley toward Coach's Place. "How about Coach's?"

He edged away from the unsound woman, not stopping until his upper arm pressed against Markie's shoulder. "No thanks. We were just heading out. Calling it a night."

Interesting. The man she'd pegged as a player just shot down another easy opportunity, again, making her rethink her assessment of him.

Tiana's nostrils flared as she bounced her gaze between Bryce and her. Her eyes narrowed and her lips pulled into a tight thin line. The woman's head ticked to the side. "Fine, then," she spat through gritted teeth.

Bryce's arm rounded over Markie's shoulders, and he pulled her tighter to his side. Heat flooded her body at his possessive hold. Yes, his action was only a front to ward off a relentless pursuer, but it felt good—right. Still, her cautious side begged her to pull away, but the hint of desire creeping through her caused her to lean into the hard, muscled body at her side.

"See ya," Bryce said as he led Markie to her car.

She didn't need to turn to verify Tiana stared after them. The woman's glare burning a hole in her back was enough to know.

Bryce yanked the driver's side door open and she slid in before he walked around the front of the vehicle and climbed in the passenger side.

"Sorry about that. I'd appreciate a ride home," Bryce commented as he stared out the windshield.

"I assumed that when you got in."

Markie thought it best to waste no time in close proximity to Tiana, so she cranked the engine, pulled out of the parking lot, and headed in the direction of Bryce's house.

"I'd planned to walk but…"

"I get it. No problem. That lady is off her rocker. You need to be careful," she warned.

"I know. I can't seem to get rid of her. And it's not like we really even dated."

"Really?" Even after what she'd just assessed about him she couldn't hold the sarcasm from her tone.

A quick glance toward him found him looking at her.

"Yes, really. And why do you have such a hard time believing me? What have I ever done for you to have such a low opinion of me when it comes to women?"

Her pulse kicked up a notch at his calling her out. She refocused on the road. "I don't."

"Well, it sure doesn't seem that way. You bust my balls every chance you get. Always making some sort of comment about me and the opposite sex."

She pulled into Bryce's driveway and flipped the car into park.

The man wasted no time reaching for the door handle. "Thanks for the ride."

"Wait!" she called out as he climbed out of the vehicle.

He bent and leaned in to see her, his face muscles taut. "What?" he asked. Annoyance emitted from his tone.

"I don't do that."

His brow arched. "Yeah, you do." He shrugged. "Whatever though. What does it matter?"

Bryce stood, shut the door, and headed up the sidewalk, soon to disappear into his house.

The cleansing breath she drew in was not cleansing. Probably would have been if Bryce's cologne hadn't pleasantly infiltrated her nostrils. Though she'd successfully ignored his tantalizing scent in the past, it had become more difficult to do so lately. That hint of sandalwood on him was like a drug. She couldn't get enough of it, and like some drug addicts she knew, she needed to kick it for her own good, but couldn't.

Markie cut the engine and flung her vehicle door open. She knocked once on his front door then turned the handle without hesitation, calling his name as she stepped inside.

He studied her from across what she presumed to be the living room, but it was hard to tell since it was in the midst of a remodel job.

"What, Markie? What do you want?" Resentful attitude still laced his tone.

"I want to explain. I don't mean to give you a hard time. Really."

He just watched her, waiting.

She swallowed hard and narrowed the gap between them, stopping just a step away from him. The heat of his body warmed hers. That sandalwood scent hit her again, and those almost black eyes of his darkened even more.

Shame caused her to pull away from that dark gaze of his. She stared at the floor. "I don't know why I do it. I'm sorry."

An outright lie. She knew darn well why she did it. She was afraid of him. Afraid of falling for him. No matter how hard she tried to tell herself he was made from the same mold as her cheating ex-fiancé, she knew the truth. He wasn't. But telling herself that kept her from putting herself out there—risking another heartbreak.

When there was still not a word from him, she drew in a deep breath, looked up, and met his gaze.

His taut facial muscles loosened. His gaze softened with each passing moment.

"Please, Bryce, just..."

His lips silenced her words and his large hands cupped her cheeks, heating her skin. His flavor seeped into her. The kiss that started as urgent slowed, calmed, teased her to the brink of uncontrolled desire. He paused, lingered, and then returned to a soft, slow seducing pace. This guy knew how to kiss.

Bryce. The guy kissing her beyond the ability to think was Bryce. How?

Shit, who cares? His lips felt so good she kept in sync with him. Could do this for hours.

Bryce pulled back. The hope it was just a pause and he'd resume faded quickly as he edged back a bit farther.

Sheer disappointment raked through her. Distance clouded over the desire in his gaze. Where was he going off to?

She took a step toward him. He took a step back and shoved his hands in his pockets. His sun-darkened face turned white.

"Are you okay?"

His gaze landed on the floor. "I'm fine. I'm sorry."

Her heart hammered. "Sorry you kissed me?"

Silence.

This certainly wasn't the behavior of a confident womanizer. "Bryce?"

He slowly lifted his gaze to meet hers. "I'm sorry, but I shouldn't have kissed you. It was a mistake. We work together. We shouldn't do this."

That was the biggest line of crap she'd ever heard. What was he afraid of? You can't kiss someone with that much emotion—heart—and not really mean it, feel it. So it couldn't be how he felt about her that made him back off just now, something else bothered him. What?

After several beats of uncomfortable silence, she fished her car keys from her pocket. "Okay then. You're probably right. This is a bad idea."

She spun around and headed for the door, holding hope he'd call after her.

Nothing.

Moving slowly, she climbed into her vehicle and started the engine, all the time wishing that front door of his would open and he'd step through it to stop her from leaving.

Nothing.

If it hadn't been for the swirling desire in his gaze when they stared at each other in silence, she wouldn't have held hope he'd come after her. Between his intense stare and the seducing movement of his mouth when it was pressed to hers, there was no way he didn't desire her. So why did he fight it?

Peeling back the layers of Bryce Hawk just became her new life mission.

Chapter Seven

The bright morning sun poked through the blinds warming Bryce's cheeks as he stared at the newly painted ceiling like he'd been doing for the past several hours. Based on the little amount of sleep he'd actually gotten, he should have just stayed up and moved on to plastering the dining room after he was finished with the living room, but instead, he mistakenly thought he'd be able to get some sleep after that mindboggling kiss he'd shared with Markie. He could have plastered this big old house in its entirety and it wouldn't have taken enough time for the effects of her kiss to wear off his lips...heart...soul.

Dammit.

This was exactly what he feared, wanting her more than he could bear. If he just hadn't kissed her he'd be okay. He would have never known the potency of it—the effect she'd have on him. He'd assumed it in the past, but now he knew for sure.

Dammit.

How in the hell was he going to manage to work at the same place as her and keep his hands off her now that he'd had a taste? To make matters worse, the emotion she poured into that kiss, and the intense look in her gaze told him she felt the same. Soulmate came to mind.

Why did I lose my control like that? Now he had to hurt her feelings, too.

He closed his eyes. Visions of Markie's milky white face and bright emerald eyes drifted through his brain. She smiled warmly. His heart fluttered. Maybe there was hope for a woman like her. Would someone like her, strong but caring, be able to accept him—his disabilities? He wanted more than anything to believe his dad that he was making too much of his disabilities. That he placed more weight on them than anyone else did. That the right woman would easily accept him for who he was. Yet every time he thought about someone—Markie—seeing his partial limb, it made him sick to know what she might think or how she might react.

Bryce opened his eyes, turned his head, and caught a glimpse of his prosthetic leg leaned up against the nightstand. Cold, hard dread weighed down his chest, making it hard to breathe. If dealing with his amputated leg wasn't bad enough already, he also had to deal with his missing testicle. *Hopeless.*

He flung the covers back, yanked the liner off the nightstand, and slipped it onto what was left of his leg, then he pulled on the prosthetic and it clicked into place.

Knowing he wasn't going to leave the house he slid into a pair of shorts and yanked a crappy, paint-stained T-shirt over his head. Today, he'd plaster the dining room. Later this week, he would paint both the living room and dining room, and then his dad could help him with cutting and staining the trim. It would be nice to complete those rooms, especially the living room. Then he could finally get his big screen TV hung and watch it from the comfort of the leather recliner he'd planned to purchase. There was lots to do yet in this big ole fixer-upper, but he enjoyed doing it as it kept his mind off things—Markie. But now, after they'd shared that kiss, pushing her to the back of his mind would be even more difficult.

Bryce stepped into the kitchen. As the coffee brewed, he leaned back against the counter and glanced around the kitchen, pleased with how it turned out. This room had been in terrible condition when he moved in, so it, along with the crappy downstairs bathroom, were the first areas he tackled. Those two rooms were far tougher than the master bedroom he completed two months ago, and the living room and dining room he currently worked on. He saved the upstairs bedrooms and bathroom for last since he really didn't need those.

Though a couple of the downstairs rooms were done, they weren't really completed, they lacked the finishing touches—warmth. The kind of warmth one sees in other houses—curtains, rugs, magnets on the fridge. When it came to that stuff, he didn't have a clue what to purchase. Maybe he could call stepmother number four for help. They were about the same age, and judging from how she'd decorated his father's house, he liked her taste. Giving his mother a call was of no use. He stopped calling her when she'd stopped returning his calls. In fact, neither he nor his brother knew where she was anymore. Overall, they made the right choice to live with their dad after the divorce, but their mom never got over it. It's not that they didn't love her, they did, but her alcoholism had been more than they could handle.

What a freaking dysfunctional family he had. An estranged alcoholic mother, a father who couldn't seem to stay married for more than a few years, and him—incomplete both physically, but more important, mentally. It's a wonder Carter turned out as good as he did. But, they all loved each other.

The coffee maker beeped and he poured himself a cup of brew.

After two mugs of coffee and a banana, he mixed a bucket of plaster and began spreading it on the walls of his dining room. He'd been at it for a couple of hours when a knock sounded on his front door. Wanting to be alone, he considered not even looking to see who it was. But the second knock got the best of him so he set down his trowel, stepped into the living room, and took a peek out the window.

Lori stood on his front step, two white bakery bags gripped in her hand. His growling stomach practically begged him to let her in. He knocked on the window, and her head snapped in his direction. He held up his pointer finger and mouthed, "Just a minute."

She nodded.

Bryce shot off to his bedroom to change out of his shorts and into a pair of jeans.

He unlocked the front door and Lori stepped through. "Morning," she said as she glanced around the room. "I just wanted to see what kind of progress you've made. It's coming along nicely."

"Thanks."

She handed him one of the bags. "I got you two of your favorites."

God, he hoped she was talking about chocolate covered, custard filled doughnuts. He opened the bag. *Awesome.* His mouth watered at the sight of them.

Lori followed him to the kitchen, pulled out a chair, and dug into her bakery bag.

"Want a cup of coffee?" he asked.

"Yeah, that'd be great."

After pouring them each a cup, he sat across from her.

He kept his eyes focused on the pastry as to avoid her usual adoring gaze and hoping to avoid giving her any false hope. He knew she liked him and wanted more than just friendship from him, and though he thought she was a great person and liked spending time with her, friendship was all he felt for her.

He did his best not to lead her on, though found himself flirting with her on occasion. He liked to flirt. It was fun for him, and he was good at it. He really missed doing it with someone he liked in a romantic way. Someone like Markie. But, when it came to flirting with her, he kept himself in check, because it was too risky—dangerous. Man, keeping in check with Markie was about the hardest thing he had to do.

Lori's warm smile reminded him he had to keep himself in check with her as well. Hurting the kind woman across the table from him was the last thing he wanted to do. She'd become a good friend.

Lori lifted her napkin and swiped it over her thin lips. Not full lips like Markie's. Not kissable lips like Markie's. His mouth and tongue tingled in anticipation of another long lingering kiss from that desirable redhead.

No. That would never happen. It couldn't.

"Are you okay?" Lori asked as she set her napkin back on her lap.

"Huh?"

"Are you okay? You look...pale."

"Yes, I'm fine. I was really givin' 'er earlier. Trying to make some headway on this place this weekend since I'll be busy for the next couple."

"Oh. You've got some exciting plans?"

"Yeah. My brother will be on leave. He's coming home for a visit, so I'm going to spend some time with him and my dad."

"That sounds nice. How are your dad and Bridget doing? They're so nice."

She'd met his dad and stepmom a few months back when they came up and took him to dinner. Lori and her parents happened to stroll into the Bay Lodge for dinner as well.

"They're good. Dad comes up every now and then and helps me out."

"That's nice he's so handy. You're both so handy. My father's a banker. Physical labor is not his thing at all," she said with a chuckle.

Her father wasn't just a banker, he was the bank president, and a nice guy to boot. He wasn't at all the stuffy old banker type.

"I almost hate to ask but..." She paused and sucked her bottom lip into her mouth as she averted her gaze momentarily. "Are the police making any headway with the murder investigations?"

Anxiety swirled in his stomach. "I don't think so, but at least Markie doesn't think it's me anymore." He swallowed hard. "I hope anyhow."

After that kiss they'd shared the night before, the way she poured emotion into it, there was no way she could possibly believe he was a murderer.

When he refocused on his guest, he noticed her eyes had narrowed, and her jaw clenched. Her nostrils constricted as she drew in a long breath. A tiny, squiggly vein swelled on her temple. He guessed she was angry Markie had considered him a person of interest. Truth be told, he was angry at the thought as well, but he realized Markie was only doing her job by investigating all leads and theories.

Her jaw loosened slightly, but her facial muscles still looked tense. "I can't believe she'd think such a thing. She knows you. She knows what a great person you are. You're the first person to raise your hand to volunteer to help someone in need. You mind your own business—"

He lifted his hand. "It's okay. She's just doing her job. It will work itself out."

"How can you be so relaxed about this? What if it doesn't? What if..."

Bryce leaned closer to her from across the table. "I will be fine. Markie's a great investigator. She'll find the murderer."

The bulging vein in Lori's temple thickened and pulsed as she ran a shaky hand through her hair. "Well, I hope for your sake the perfect little Markie Pearson does."

The hostility lacing her tone surprised him. Had she read him? Did she know of his romantic feelings for Markie? Was it jealousy that upset her? He'd never seen her even slightly angry. She was always the bubbly, perky type, but right now, the level of anger laced in her tight facial muscles and emitting from her stare alarmed him.

Her gaze drifted to the window for a few ticks before she crumpled up her napkin and stuffed it into the bakery bag lying on the table.

Her facial muscles softened, then she glanced around the room. "Well, I guess I should let you get back to it."

The comment was the kind as if looking for an invitation to stay longer, and though he didn't mind her company, he wanted to get back to work.

"Yeah, those walls don't plaster themselves."

She rose slowly as if still waiting for an invite to hang around. Asking her to stay would be a mistake, not to mention a little uncomfortable in her present mood.

"You have a lot of work to be done here. I could help you," Lori offered.

"Thanks. I appreciate that but mudding is a one person job," he countered.

"Oh, okay."

This conversation—visit—needed to end. He sprang to his feet. "Thanks so much for the doughnuts. They hit the spot."

"You're welcome."

She smiled and nodded as he walked past her to lead her out.

He opened the front door for her.

Glancing over her shoulder, she caught his gaze. "If you want to do something later, when you're done for the day, some of the dart league group is getting together at O'Malley's to shoot a few rounds."

"Thanks. But I think I'm going to work late. Finish up some stuff."

Disappointment emitted from her gaze. "Okay. But if you change your mind you know where to find us."

He closed the door behind her, spun around, and leaned back. If Lori didn't find someone else to focus her energy on soon he'd probably have to quit the dart league to distance himself from her.

* * *

"Exactly who are you hoping to see tonight?" Her best friend asked.

Markie turned and looked at her to find her knowing, inquisitive gaze nearly smiling. "Huh?"

"Hmm, let's see. You're wearing eye shadow, which happens rarely, the earrings are even rarer. You've looked in the mirror at least ten times in the past five minutes. And don't even get me started on the fact you curled your hair. I didn't even know you owned a curling iron let alone knew how to style *going out* hair."

Her cheeks heated. She could lie to her friend about hoping she'd see Bryce at O'Malley's tonight, but she wasn't good at lying, and her bestie would see through anything she made up. They'd been friends for too many years for her to hide the truth.

After a few ticks of the clock, Amber filled the silence. "Fine. Keep your little secret for now. I'll figure it out."

"Can we just go?"

"Sure."

They loaded into Amber's car and headed to O'Malley's.

Typical for a Saturday night, the parking lot was nearly full. Markie's heart skipped a beat at the sight of Lori Holloway's car parked near the entrance. If she was in there, perhaps the entire dart team was as well. They were a tight group. It likely meant that Bryce was in there, too.

She and Amber slipped through the back door and squeezed their way through the crowd until they reached the bar. They each ordered a mug of beer.

Markie lifted the glass to her lips as she scanned over the top of the rim to scope out the clientele. Sure enough, Lori and some of her teammates were sitting at a table near the dartboards. No Bryce, though. Maybe he just wasn't here yet.

Her friend shouldered her. "I wonder if that hottie Bryce is here."

Markie's pulse picked up at the sound of his name. "Probably. The rest of his dart team is here," she said, making every effort to keep her tone in check so her comrade wouldn't figure her out.

Every man's gazes were on Amber as she moved toward the dartboards. She reached out and grabbed her model-grade friend's upper arm. "Where are you going?"

Her friend's eyebrows drew together. "Over by Bryce's gang."

This wasn't the first time her bestie had made reference to Bryce being a hottie, or the first time she intentionally placed herself in his line of sight. But so far, the city planner hadn't taken the bait.

"Oh."

"You don't want to go over there?"

Of course she did. That's why she was out tonight in the first place. Since O'Malley's was their league sponsor, his team hung out there regularly. This was a way to see Bryce and attempt to be discreet about it.

She released her friend's thin arm and followed her. "Yeah, I guess it's okay."

Amber stepped up between Phil and Doug; both immediately offered their chairs to her. She passed on the offers as she stepped around the other side of the tall table and stood between Lori and Mike. Lori scooted her chair over a bit.

"Heard you guys are doing well in the league," Amber commented.

"Yeah, we're in first but only by a few games," Phil responded with a proud smile.

"Makes sense with as much as you guys seem to practice," she replied.

The guy just smiled.

"No Bryce tonight?" Amber asked.

"Nope." Lori hissed out. The woman's facial muscles tightened.

Why Lori's tenseness at the simple question? Jealousy?

"Hmm, that's odd," Amber commented.

"He's home. Working on his house." Lori fixed her glare on Markie. "I think that was just an excuse though. If I had to guess, I'd say he's hiding, staying out of the public eye because the whole town knows he's a murder suspect." the woman's shrill tone held no secrets.

The table fell silent. In fact, the blasting music and fifty other conversations in the bar fell silent to Markie's ears as well. Her pounding pulse was all she heard.

"Now wait just a minute, Markie is only doing her job." Amber defended.

Lori raised her hand in the stop position. "I don't want to hear it," she said as she swung her gaze from Amber to her. The woman's nostrils flared. "You know him. He would never do anything like that. I don't know why you always have to give him such a hard time."

Markie hitched her chin. "Hard time. I don't. My job is to find out who killed Sister Ann and Edwin

Hulbert, and that includes following all leads no matter who they may involve."

She pulled her gaze from Lori and planted it on her bestie. "This is why I don't go out in this town. All I wanted was a couple of beers and to have some fun. Not listen to this."

It was time to leave. She needed to walk away before this escalated. It wouldn't look good for a police investigator to get into an argument in a bar. Something like that would spread like wildfire in this small town, probably wind up on the front page of the newspaper, and explode on social media. Both she and the department didn't need that crap. Plus, she didn't want to hear any more about how she gave Bryce a hard time. Too much truth, and for that she was ashamed and embarrassed.

Amber looked at Markie over the roof of her car. "I'm sorry. If I'd known Lori would go all bat-shit crazy like that I would have never gone over to her table."

"It's okay. You couldn't have known."

"What an odd outburst from her. Don't you think? She never acts that way," her friend said, then slipped into the vehicle.

Markie opened the passenger door and slid in. "I know. It did seem strange."

Amber cranked the engine. "Did you want to go somewhere else?"

"Just home."

After the short ride back to her place, and still in need of a drink, she invited her bestie inside. They each popped a beer.

Amber zoned in on her. "I guess I've always known Lori had a thing for Bryce, but good Lord she seemed really angry at you. Lucky for you eyes can't really shoot daggers."

In acknowledgment, she nodded and took another swig from her bottle.

"I can't imagine what she'd be like if he actually showed any interest in her. She'd probably turn into one of those femme fatale's." Amber stated.

They shared a chuckle, though a part of her didn't find it funny.

"So, you going to tell me who you got all dolled up for?"

Markie shook her head. "I just wanted to go out and have a nice time."

Her friend's head tilted to the side. "Okay, you just keep your little secret for now, but you know I'll find out eventually."

Markie knew she'd better watch her step around Amber. Her best friend was intuitive. Probably already knew it was Bryce who sent her heart racing which was why she'd dashed over to the dart team's table at the bar—force her to face Bryce if he showed. But with as many times as she had spouted off to her comrade that she thought he was a casanova, she was too embarrassed to tell her how much she'd grown to like the man.

Pressing her fingers to her lips, she recalled the kiss she and Bryce shared the night before. That sweet, lingering kiss that had been on her mind the entire day. The kiss that led her to call her friend to go out in hopes to find Bryce at the bar. The kiss that kept her awake the entire night fantasizing about what could follow a sensual kiss like that.

Her chest hollowed as she remembered Bryce's retraction. She couldn't believe he let her walk away last night after that mindboggling kiss. Hope filled the empty space in her heart as she recalled the desire that swirled in his gaze right before she turned away from him to leave. Yet, with all that yearning and want in his eyes, he still let her leave.

Next time, Bryce Hawk. Next time I'm not going to let you off the hook so easily.

Chapter Eight

Bryce climbed between the crisp sheets of his king-sized bed and stared into the darkness as he debated if he'd made the right choice by doing an about-face the second he saw Markie step through the back door of O'Malley's earlier. Odd, he'd come through the front door at the very same moment. Even though he'd declined Lori's offer, something caused him to quit working on his house an hour earlier, clean up, and walk to O'Malley's.

When he closed his eyes Markie's angelic face, sprinkled with those sexy, reddish-brown freckles, appeared on the back of his eyelids. Her hair had looked different tonight. Made-up. Soft, shiny red curls framed her face. And her clothes. The short, hot-pink skirt was not the attire she normally wore. The sight of her pale, shapely legs, and pink painted toenails had sent his heart into overdrive. The woman had the face and body of an angel. More importantly, she had the soul of one.

His stubby limb twitched, reminding him he'd never get and keep hold of a woman like that.

Click.

Bryce popped open his eyes and sprang into a seated position. *What was that?*

Back door? No. Service door to the garage?

He swung his leg over the side of the bed and yanked his pistol from the drawer of the nightstand, then he reached for his prosthetic leg.

Before he could grip it, the house shook, hard, jostling everything from within reach while tossing him to the floor. His ears rang from the explosion.

79

Pain ripped through his ghostly limb. Memories of dirt, rocks, and shrapnel pelting and penetrating his body shot through his mind.

Is this a memory or really happening?

The pain tearing through his flesh felt real—familiar.

When the scent of smoke snapped him back into reality, he found himself curled in the fetal position on his carpeted bedroom floor. Automatically, he reached for his leg. Gone. His heart leaped into his throat. Wait, of course it was. Fear froze him in place. What if he reached for the other and it wasn't there? The smoke filling his lungs caused him to choke. His eyes watered. His shaky hands reached for his other leg. Warmth of his own touch assured him it was still there and sent a message that he'd better pull it together and get to safety.

With the thickening smoke, he was unable to find his prosthetic leg but did manage to grasp the hand grip of one of his crutches that had been leaning against the wall collecting dust.

He made his way to the bedroom door and gripped the scorching doorknob. His fingers sprang open, palm burned. He wasn't getting out that way. He hobbled toward the window. His toe caught under something unrecognizable. Hands flailing like a madman he fell to the floor. Luckily, his knee broke the face-forward fall.

Glass sliced into his hands as he crawled across the floor.

Sirens echoed in the distance, growing louder with each passing moment. He welcomed the deafening noise.

After a few more clumsy movements, he reached out and touched the windowsill. Gripping the warm wood, he pulled himself up and flung his body out the window, then he rolled away from the house.

"Are you okay?" someone asked.

He lay on his back in the cool grass, gasping for fresh air. His lungs burned, pain shot through his wet hands. *Moisture? Probably blood.*

"Bryce. Help is on the way. Can you hear me?"

"Robert?"

"Yes. Jesus, what happened?"

Bryce tried to focus on his neighbor. "I don't know," he whispered through his burning throat.

Robert helped him to a seated position. Flames shot out of his bedroom window. His house was a goner along with the rest of his stuff.

His coughing began to subside and his cloudy vision began to clear enough that he could see his sliced up bloody hands.

A firefighter and two paramedics ran toward him. One firefighter barked out orders and others scrambled around the trucks, opening doors, pulling hoses, and pushing buttons.

The paramedics helped him to the ambulance and took his vitals. His pulse and blood pressure were through the roof. They hoisted him onto a cot, lifted it into the ambulance, and hooked him to oxygen.

One of the EMTs inspected his hands. "Not too bad. You'll probably need a couple of stitches on your palm.

"Are you okay?"

He lifted his head and looked at Captain Tomie. The man wore a T-shirt and jeans. Not his usual attire. He must have grabbed the nearest clothes he could find and ran out of his house when he'd heard the 911 call.

"Yeah."

Tomie ran his gaze over him, lingering for a moment at his leg, or lack thereof. The man offered an understanding nod. Until now, he and Chief Mertz were the only two people in town who knew about his leg. The subject had come up shortly after he started at City Hall and for some reason he'd chosen to reveal it to the men. Maybe it was because they'd both served in the military as well and he knew they'd have a sense of understanding. A tinge of liberation washed over him when he disclosed it to them, especially since he knew they'd keep his secret.

"What happened?"

Bryce laid his heavy head back down. "I don't know. I was in bed and the house just exploded."

His body quivered at the thought of his near death experience.

"Is anyone else inside?"

He heard the Captain ask him a question but he couldn't process his words. His brain was mush.

"Huh?"

"Is there anybody else in the house?"

Was anyone? Had that been the door he heard click right before the explosion?

The large lump of anxiety in his throat was nearly impossible to swallow down. Had someone come into his house and set off the explosion? "I...don't know."

The concerned man leaned over him. "You don't know?"

"I was in bed, and I swear to God I heard the service door to the garage click. I was getting up to check it out when the house exploded. So if someone came in, I don't know if they were on their way in or out, then the explosion occurred."

"Is he okay?"

Markie's voice came through all the noise and chaos outside the ambulance. His heart warmed at the concern laced in her tone.

Needing to see her warm, emerald eyes, he pushed himself up on his elbows. One quick glimpse at where his leg used to be caused his pulse to race faster. Anxiety ripped through him. He couldn't let her see him like this.

He flung his gaze to Captain Tomie. "Don't let her in here!"

Without hesitation, Tomie jumped out of the ambulance and shut the door.

Bryce breathed out a sigh of relief. It was as if the man immediately understood why he didn't want to see Markie. He pulled his gaze from the doors and shifted it to his legs—leg. How in the hell was he going to keep this from people—her—until he could get a new prosthetic leg.

"We're going to get you up to the ER," stated the EMT who'd been looking at his hands.

With a nod, he eased back down.

It had taken less than an hour for the ER doctor to stitch up his palm and put some ointment on the burns on his hands from the doorknob. The forced oxygen was a blessing to his lungs as much as the drops were to his itchy eyes. It seemed with every fresh breath he took, the soreness in his throat subsided along with the dryness. By the time Captain Tomie popped into his room, he felt pretty good except for coping with the fact his house was surely a total loss. The house he'd been working so hard on.

"Is there anyone you want to call before they see it on the news? You can use my phone, or I can make the call if you'd like?"

"No. I'll call my dad in the morning. No sense in ruining his sleep."

"Markie wants in here. She's pretty relentless and may shoot her way in if I don't let her see you soon."

Bryce's chest tightened. He'd done so well at keeping his secret from her—everyone, until now.

The compassionate man leaned toward him. "Bryce, this isn't the end of the world."

His fatherly tone was both knowing and reassuring.

"Of course not, I can get another house."

"Nice try, but you know I'm not talking about the house."

Confirmation the man knew for sure how he felt about Markie and that he wanted to keep his secret from her. Bryce stared at the wall.

"Well, that aside, we need to figure out what happened tonight and why. Chief Bosley will call in the state fire marshal in the morning."

Again, he told him what little he knew, and at present, they had no answers to the most evident questions. Was the explosion intentional? If so, who tried to kill him? And, was it the same person who killed his property maintenance violators?

* * *

Markie paced the hospital hall, waiting for word from Captain Tomie about Bryce. Yes, she knew his injuries were minor, but she still needed to see him to make sure. She'd been seconds too late to the scene. In fact, she was about to climb into the back of the ambulance when the captain shot out, shut the door, and slapped his palm against the metal, indicating the ambulance should go.

As for Bryce's house, that was a total loss. All his hard work for nothing.

Her gut clenched. Deep down she knew this wasn't an accident. Someone set off that explosion. Who would do such a thing, want to...a quiver raked through her nearly knocking her off her feet...who would want to kill Bryce and why?

When she reached the end of the hall she spun around to walk back toward the ER. Only she and Captain were at the hospital. Chief Mertz and the on-duty police officers were at the scene with Fire Chief Bosley and his crew. Come hell or high water, she was going to figure out who did this and make sure justice would be served.

From down the hall, she caught the captain slipping through the ER doors. The grim look he wore earlier had been replaced with a slightly less worried expression. That had to be good, still, she picked up her pace.

"Is he okay?"

"Minor burns on his hands and arms, a few cuts, nothing a couple of stitches didn't take care of, and he's being treated for smoke inhalation. Luckily that wasn't too bad either."

"Can I see him?"

His gaze stayed on her. "Not tonight. He needs his rest. I'm going to come back later in the morning and talk with him some more. He's tired and groggy."

I'm. He said I'm. Did that mean she was not to join him even though *she* was the investigator assigned to the possible related murder cases?

"Well, shouldn't I…"

He held up his hand. "I'm going to talk to him in the morning for starters. Go home and get some rest."

"But…"

He moved his hand a bit closer to her.

Chain of command. Markie reminded herself. She loathed the hierarchy at this particular moment and craved for a way around it.

"Yes sir."

She turned and mentally huffed away.

On her way home, she drove past Bryce's house—what was left of it. Firefighters still scrambled around the wreckage. Neighbors lined the sidewalk filming the disaster with their phones. The poor guy's unfortunate incident was probably already plastered all over social media. Nothing was sacred anymore.

She pulled into her driveway, cut the engine, and let her sluggish feet carry her to the front door. She slipped into the house, made a beeline to her bedroom, and flopped down face-first onto the bed. Exhaustion consumed her.

Upon waking, she found herself in the exact position as where she collapsed earlier in the wee morning hours. When the sleep cleared out of her eyes, she narrowed in on the clock. Half past seven. Though she'd only gotten five hours of sleep, she rolled out of bed and headed to the bathroom. A quick shower to wake her up was needed, then she'd scoot back up to the hospital to see Bryce, ignoring the captain's orders. Sort of, anyhow.

She arrived at the hospital within the hour to find he had been moved from the ER to a private room. His stepmother stood outside the doorway, leaning against the wall. Her thumbs tapped against her phone.

She'd met the young lady, not much older than Bryce, a few months back when she and Bryce's dad stopped in at City Hall. Since then, she'd seen her a couple of times, but never really talked with her.

Bridget glanced up and smiled warmly. "Markie, right?"

"Yes. How are you?"

The petite woman shrugged. "Better now than we first got here. William was a mess until he found out Bryce was fine. Just some cuts and bruises."

"I suppose he was worried."

"Yeah. I stepped out of the room so they could talk a bit. Bryce doesn't open up a lot, only to his dad. Though he's fine physically, he's still having a rough time of it." Bridget paused and turned toward her, "Do you really think someone did this on purpose? That's what Bryce thinks."

"I don't know. When I leave here, I'm going to meet my captain so we can try to figure out what happened. Hopefully, we can quickly get someone up here from the State Fire Marshal's office to start investigating."

The door opened, drawing Markie's attention. Bryce's dad stepped through. His gaze fixed on her. "Good morning."

"Morning. Can I go in and see Bryce?"

The man stared at her for a couple of seconds before swinging his gaze to his wife. The young lady shrugged hesitantly.

Why on earth was everyone afraid to let her in by Bryce? First the captain last night, and now his dad and stepmom.

Her pulse quickened. Was he worse off than what they'd let on? Had he been disfigured by the fire?

"I...let me check with him," Bryce's dad said as he spun to reenter the room.

Looking over William's shoulder she could only see the foot of Bryce's bed and a set of crutches leaning against the wall before the door clicked shut.

Markie looked at Bridget, "Did Bryce hurt his foot or leg last night."

"No, not that I'm aware of."

"Oh, I saw some crutches in there."

Bryce's stepmom's gaze landed on the floor.

"Bridget, what's going on?"

The woman slowly lifted her head. "I can't say, it's not my story to tell. I would but he's so...I don't know, I guess dead set against talking about it."

Markie blew out an exaggerated breath. What was with all this secrecy? "Screw it. I'm going in," she said as she made a move for the door.

Bridget leaped in front of her. "Please don't. He's just not ready yet...my heart breaks for him."

The desperation in the woman's gaze and tone froze Markie in place. The shared stare felt like it lasted an eternity.

"I just want to see him. Make sure he's okay. I know you said it but..." Markie swallowed down the lump in her throat. "I care about him."

"I know you do. I can see it in your eyes. And Bryce cares for you as well. My husband's told me. And that's what makes it even harder for him."

"I don't understand."

The door opened again and William stepped out. He looked ragged, unlike minutes ago when he greeted her with a little morning sunshine.

Her heart sank. "I take it he doesn't want to see me?" Markie asked.

"No. Though I don't know why. His secret will come out anyhow. There will be no hiding it when he returns to work tomorrow." The distraught man ran his hand through his thinning gray hair. "My son will hate me for this, but I think you should go in anyhow. However, I need to warn you about something first."

Secret? Her heart leaped into her throat. *How bad is this? What is he hiding?*

William shared an apprehensive look with his wife. Bridget nodded.

The older gentleman cleared his throat. "While Bryce was with the Marines in Afghanistan several years back, his truck ran over an improvised explosive device. He was injured pretty bad." The weathered man paused and blew out a breath. "He lost his left leg just below the knee and suffered some other injuries. His leg being the most obvious."

Markie just stared at him. Had she heard him correctly? Bryce had worked at City Hall for a couple of years already, how could she not know he'd suffered that kind of significant injury? This would explain that little limp she saw on occasion. Thinking back, she'd never seen him in shorts. He intentionally hid it. Why?

"So, he wears a prosthetic leg?"

William nodded. "He lost it in the explosion last night and it will take a while to get another."

Markie wasn't sure what to say next. She still didn't understand why this was such a problem. The way he acted she began to wonder if he was embarrassed, ashamed of it?

Oh my, he is.

Guilt washed over her for how she'd sometimes treated him in the past. How she'd busted his chops simply for the fun of it. Took her own problems out on him just because he reminded her of her ex when he had enough of his own problems.

"I'm sorry, William, but I just don't understand. He let Captain Tomie in, why not me."

He cracked a half-smile. "Bryce probably doesn't really care what the man thinks about what he feels is a disability. He's not in love with Captain Tomie."

Her heart slammed against her ribcage. *Love.* Was Bryce's dad really saying what she thought?

The soft-spoken man's gaze stayed on her. "I've been trying to get him to move on with life, but he still has a tough time of it. He's probably not going to be happy with me for telling you about this, but he'll get over it and forgive me eventually. I'm not going to stand in your way of going through this door," he said as he pointed to Bryce's room.

Markie made a move for the door.

"Wait!" Bridget exclaimed.

Both she and Bryce's dad looked at her.

"William?" Bridget said his name as she tilted her head to the side, and gave him an urging look as if he should be saying more.

"Bryce needs to tell her the rest," William said.

The man paused, fixed his attention on Markie, and cleared his throat. "Just keep in mind, losing his leg wasn't his only injury. Please be patient with him."

Patience wasn't her thing, but the seriousness in William's eyes urged her to try. Though she wasn't sure what other injury the man referred to.

She pushed her way through the large door and immediately caught Bryce's wide-eyed gape. His mouth was opening to protest so she hurried over, framed his flaming cheeks in her hands, and pressed her lips to his. So much for her patience, but it was the only way she could think of to keep him from kicking her out of the room. She kissed him softly and refused to stop until she was sure he wouldn't ask her to leave.

His mouth moved with hers. When his bandaged hands cupped her cheeks she knew she was close to her desired outcome. She kissed him a bit longer, then inched back only to be drawn back in by him for a few seconds longer.

She pulled back but held his hands in hers. "I'm so glad you're okay. I was so worried about you."

"I'll be fine. They're springing me loose today if everything checks out with the doctor this morning."

She eyed the little scrape on his cheekbone surrounded by a hint of purplish bruising. Her fingers itched to trace it—wipe it away, but she knew she'd better play her cards carefully as to not alienate him.

"Where are you going to go?" she asked.

"I'll get a hotel room. Figure shit out." He half-smiled. "Get some clothes."

The poor guy lost everything. Escaped only with the clothes on his back.

"I'm so sorry this happened to you."

"It'll be fine."

"You can stay at my house for a while, 'til you figure things out."

Bryce's apprehensive gaze laced with a hint of distress settled on his mattress. Even under the covers, it was easy to see he was missing his leg. He sucked his lips into his mouth. His eyes glazed over.

She thought it best to wait him out. Let him stay in control of this moment.

After a few beats, he cleared his throat. "Thanks, Markie. I appreciate it, but I don't want to put you out."

"It's no problem."

He shook his head. "No. I can't."

His words were firming up. William's reference to patience replayed through her mind. She'd better let him win this battle or she'd only shove him further away.

"Okay. Well, you know you can call me if you need me."

She returned her attention to the large, scraped up hands in hers. "Couple stitches, huh."

"Yeah. I'm lucky that was it."

"I'm going to meet Captain Tomie and the fire marshal at your place in a bit. I take it your dad is coming back to help you get settled."

"Yeah."

She leaned forward and pressed her lips lightly to his. "Please call me if you need anything."

"Okay."

Walking out of that room was one of the hardest things she ever had to do. She wanted to hug that strong-willed man and whisper to him that everything would be okay. Tell him whatever his injuries were, it didn't matter to her. She'd fallen for him already on what she did know about him. He was a smart, kind, caring man, and any woman would be lucky to get someone like him.

But he wasn't meant for just any woman. He was meant for her.

Chapter Nine

Anxiety pinned Bryce in the driver's seat of his rental vehicle in the City Hall parking lot. He got there early in hopes to hobble in on his crutches before anyone else arrived. He planned to spend the whole day in his office, behind his desk, so that the employees who didn't already know about his leg wouldn't find out today. The last thing he needed or wanted was that old familiar pitying look he received from people when they found out about his leg. It was already going to be bad enough today because of his situation with his house, he didn't need to make matters any worse.

He flung open his door and made his way into the building without seeing anyone. *Perfect.*

He plopped into his chair and looked at his aching hands. They hurt badly enough to begin with, but to have to use them to crutch his way everywhere added insult to injury. *Suck it up. It could have been a lot worse.*

Ten minutes later, other staff began to filter in. Most stopping by his office to talk about his house and offer help. Admittedly, this was exactly why he loved this small town. Yeah, it could be tough that everyone knew your business, and it was hard to hide something when you wanted to—like an amputated leg—but on the flipside, everyone got to know everyone and were more than willing to lend a hand when needed.

The genuine kindness of his coworkers had him wondering if he wasn't being absolutely ridiculous in trying to hide out in his office all day to conceal the fact he'd lost his leg. It could be weeks before he got a new prosthetic. Knowing he needed to face the fact there would be no way he could hide it that long, he blew out an accepting, heavy sigh.

By the time noon rolled around he was dying to see his house, what was left of it anyhow. He sucked in a deep breath, grabbed his crutches, and headed for his vehicle. He dreaded having to crutch his way through City Hall—expose the secret of his missing leg, but he had no choice if he wanted to go look at his house. He hoped the insurance adjuster had been there already so they could get started on a housing plan.

Sweat beaded on his brow and his pulse raced as he walked past the reception desk. Mary looked up, and he informed her he'd be gone a bit longer than normal today. Her gaze ran over him.

His jaw clenched at her double-take. He forced himself to relax. "Yes, I wear a prosthetic leg. It got ruined in the fire," Bryce said, working hard to keep a steady—normal tone. He was kind of glad it was Mary he had to tell first. She was a nice woman, the grandmotherly type, and she probably wouldn't make a big deal about it.

"I never noticed that. I hope you're able to get another one soon. Our insurance company is pretty good about it. My husband broke his last year while waterskiing. We thought maybe they'd give him a little grief about it. You know, being a sport he probably shouldn't be doing. They covered without a word. Still though, I can't tell my husband anything, he just keeps doing what he does. Let me know if you need any help with the insurance." She winked. "I've got some experience there."

Relief sifted through him. Yes, for sure he was glad Mary was first.

"Thank you. I'll be back shortly."

He'd just about made it out the back door when he ran into City Administrator Johnston.

"Jeez, you're actually here today?" Johnston said as his gaze ran the length of him.

Bryce suspected everyone he'd run into would do the same thing. The old once-over. Who could blame them?

"Yeah. There's nothing I can do yet. Hopefully, I'll see the insurance adjuster today."

Johnston didn't ask about his leg, and he didn't offer anything up. He supposed the news would travel fast now at City Hall, as fast if not faster than the news of the fire. Ha, it would travel fast as wildfire. Bryce smiled at his own lame joke.

"Bryce, if you need time off, take it. And if there's anything I can do to help don't hesitate to ask."

"Thank you."

He continued to his car. Maybe it wouldn't be so bad, everyone finding out about his leg. But what about Markie. What would she think? Her opinion—approval—was the one he needed most, feared the most.

Near his home, he noted Fire Chief Bosley's truck and the State Fire Marshal's vehicle parked on the street. His driveway was cluttered with debris, mostly bricks that once shaped his old house. His lungs drained. Maybe it wasn't an old family homestead, but it was his, and it contained a lot of sweat equity.

He parked behind the chief, flung his door open, steadied himself on his crutches, then stood on the street for a moment, eyeing the heap that had once been his home. It reminded him of Dorothy's house in the *Wizard of Oz* as if picked up from its foundation and dropped to the ground in a crooked, haphazard heap. Only his house was charred as well.

"Bryce," his neighbor yelled from his front step.

A big, construction worker looking guy stood next to Robert. The man held a clipboard. They walked toward him as he made his way toward them.

Robert offered a sympathetic nod. "I'm glad to see you up and around."

"Thanks. Nothing too major. Just some cuts and burns on my hands." Bryce said as he stole a quick glimpse of his sore hands.

His neighbor gestured toward the man next to him. "This is Freddie from Berkhan Construction. He's just checking out my house—the foundation—to make sure everything is okay. Christ, I can't imagine what it was like for you judging from the way my house shook."

Anxiety swirled in his stomach. He still didn't know why his house exploded, but if it had been intentional, ultimately, he realized the danger to his neighbors as well.

"Gosh, I hope everything is okay," he said.

Robert looked at Freddie. "So far everything is checking out just fine. Matt's house looks good, too."

Matt was his neighbor on the other side. Thank goodness the lots were fairly large in this old section of town.

The chief and marshal stepped out from around the back of the house.

"Well, I'd better go see if they've found out what caused the explosion."

The men nodded and Bryce walked away.

Chief Bosley looked at him grimly.

The news wasn't going to be good.

"Did you find the cause of the explosion?" Bryce asked.

"Yeah. Looks like a pipe bomb in the garage. I think when it exploded some shrapnel may have pierced your gas cans, and the tank of your vehicle, igniting the liquid, and causing the flames to spread more quickly. The bomb itself didn't look that large, but certainly large enough. I need to study it some more," the fire marshal said.

The air drained from his lungs. His fingers tightened around the hand grips of his crutches. Someone really did try to kill him. But who? Why? He kind of figured this was the case, from the moment he'd heard the service door to the garage click in the middle of the night. But to hear him say this was intentional was truly eerie and disturbing.

"We'll know more soon. I'll keep in touch," the chief said before he and the marshal turned to leave.

In disbelief, he stared at the rubble he once called a home.

"Are you feeling okay?" his dad asked as he and his stepmom stepped beside him.

He hadn't even heard them drive up.

Was he? No. He'd just found out for sure someone tried to kill him. No. He wasn't okay. *Who in the hell would try to kill me?*

"Bryce?"

"I just found out they think the explosion was intentional."

"Oh my God," Bridget gasped.

His father slung an arm around his stepmom's shoulders and pulled her tight to his side. "Do they know who did it?" his dad asked.

He shook his head.

"What are they going to do about protection for you?"

"Not sure."

"Maybe you should come and stay with us. Get out of here for now."

"No. I don't know."

Over his dad's shoulder, Bryce caught a glimpse of Markie climbing out of the captain's SUV. "Dammit!"

"What?" his dad asked as he craned his neck to look over his shoulder in the direction Bryce stared.

"It's Markie. She's here." He grimaced down at his foot. His entire body tensed.

His stepmom placed a comforting hand on his shoulder. "You couldn't hide this from her forever. Plus, she already knows."

His pulse raced. "What? How?"

When his father wouldn't look at him, he had his answer.

"You told her? Her of all people." His voice raised with each syllable.

His dad lifted his gaze. "Well, you wouldn't see her. She was worried about you…"

"It wasn't your business to tell." Bryce's jaw clenched so hard he could barely finish his sentence.

"Not my business? You're my son, my business. I just want you to get past this, and open yourself to happiness."

"Bryce, she doesn't care," Bridget piped in.

He glared at her. How dare she weigh-in. She was just another in the line of his stepmothers. The *fourth* one. She didn't have a clue as to what he was going through, and who knew how long she'd be around? She had no right to comment.

She looked down. "Sorry."

Bryce eyed his dad. "How could you?"

"You know, Bridget is right. Markie doesn't care."

"How would you know that?"

"I saw the way she kissed you at the hospital."

"You what?"

Bryce's heart thudded and his lips tingled as he recalled that magnificent, desperately needed kiss. In the next split second, his heart nearly cracked in half at the thought of never getting another kiss from Markie's glorious, full red lips again now that she'd know his secret.

"When she went into your room after I talked with her in the hallway. Women don't kiss men that way if they're not all in...and she knew about your leg when she did that."

"She probably did it out of sympathy," he shot back. "Thanks," he added sarcastically.

His dad threw his hands in the air, spun to leave, and then turned back around. "You know what? I'm done with this! Go ahead, live your life lonely!"

As his father stomped off, Bryce wanted to kick himself. The one person who'd stuck by his side through thick and thin seemed to be the one person he kept giving a hard time to.

Bridget hesitated to follow. Compassion, not anger, lined her gaze. "He just loves you so much."

Now he felt even worse. More like a disappointment.

"I know."

"I'll get him to come back in a little bit," she assured him.

"Thanks. I appreciate that."

"And Bryce."

"Yes."

"Like your dad said, Markie knew about your leg before she kissed you like her life depended on it. Give her a chance. Don't let a good one like that slip away."

She had a point. Maybe Markie could see beyond his disability. But his leg was the least of his disabilities. How would she react to a man who may not be able to…perform—satisfy—a woman?

Sweat beaded on his brow as his stepmother walked away and Markie approached. Thank goodness she stopped to talk with the captain for a second or she probably would have heard him and his dad's awful exchange.

Markie's gaze held his. He figured she'd lower it to his leg like everyone else did, but she didn't. The intenseness of her stare lit every nerve ending in his body. Those bright emerald eyes bore right into his soul.

On one hand, he wanted to spin and leave, on the other, he wanted a kiss from those full red lips. The lips that twice now had sent his heart racing.

"How are you feeling today?"

"I'm fine."

She nodded. "I heard you were at work today. I wanted to see you sooner, but I've been out of the office all morning."

"No worries."

Off in the distance, Captain Tomie finished his conversation with the fire chief and fire marshal and headed toward him and Markie.

"Hey, Bryce," Tomie said.

"Hey."

"So, I know you already know this was a deliberate action."

His stomach flopped. Yes, he already knew, but he still wasn't used to hearing it.

Markie reached out and wrapped her delicate fingers around his upper arm. "We'll find out who did this."

Of course she would. She was a great investigator, but would she find out before... Bryce swallowed hard. Before it was too late for him.

"Markie's right. But for the time being, I think you should stay with someone, not at the hotel, for your safety," Captain Tomie said.

"I suppose I could go stay with my dad." He only wished he hadn't just pissed him off.

Tomie bounced his gaze between him and Markie. "I was thinking more like with Markie."

Adrenaline whipped through Bryce's veins. Using his hand, he swiped the sweat from his brow. He couldn't stay with her, couldn't risk being that close to her.

Markie's grip tightened on his arm. "I think it's for the best right now."

"You could stay with me," the kind man offered. "But it's total chaos with my kids, and my in-laws are here. But if you'd rather, you can."

No. He couldn't disrupt the man's family like that. Maybe he could stay with the chief. No, that wouldn't work. The police chief was headed out of town.

Shit.

No, absolutely not. He wasn't going to stay with Markie. He could protect himself. No, he couldn't do that either because his handgun was in his house which was now burned to a crisp.

That's it, he was going to his dad's.

No, he couldn't do that either. It wasn't fair to bring this danger to his father and stepmother.

Shit.

He had no option but to stay with Markie. With her being a cop, she would be prepared to protect him and herself from the killer. But with that proximity, how would he be able to protect her, and himself—shield his heart from her.

Bryce fixed his gaze on Markie.

"So it's settled then," she said.

"I guess."

* * *

Markie pulled into her two stall garage, then motioned for Bryce to do the same. He climbed out of his rental, grabbed his crutches, and his bag of clothes and necessities he'd purchased earlier in the day. The somber look on his face had been there all day. But she could hardly fault him for that. He'd lost everything. And now he was forced to stay with her. Judging from the way he had kissed her, she knew it shouldn't be a total hardship for him, but the distraught look on his face sure displayed a different story.

Bryce wobbled on his crutches. Instinctively, she reached toward him to help, and he flinched like he'd touched a hot stove. She reeled her arm back. Though she wanted to help him with the bag he carried, she thought better of it. This independent man wanted no help from anyone. Up until now, he'd done an excellent job of hiding the fact he wore a prosthetic leg. She felt bad for him, his secret was out. But, to her, she didn't completely understand why it was such a problem with him that people knew he'd lost his leg. It didn't change the man he was. At any rate, for now, she'd do her best to not bring attention to it.

Thank goodness, they'd stayed at work later than usual. It was almost seven o'clock by the time they'd left. She didn't know how they'd fill the evening alone as awkward as Bryce seemed to feel about staying with her.

Every time she caught glimpses of those dark, sexy eyes of his, she had visions about how they could spend the evening, but she guessed with all that had gone on with him the past week what she had in mind was probably furthest from his mind.

Turning away from him she led the way into the house. She flipped on the kitchen light and looked over her shoulder at him. "My mom called earlier. She heard some scuttlebutt about what happened to you. She fixes everything with food, so she dropped off some pork ribs and potatoes for us. Do you like that?"

"Yeah, that'd be great."

She pointed down the hall. "The spare room is on the right, just past the bathroom. I'll let you get settled in."

Bryce nodded and made his way down the hall.

Markie pulled the containers out of the fridge. Her mother had put a little sticky note on the lid. *Enjoy. Let me know if you need anything else. And let your friend know how sorry we are about his troubles.*

She smiled and silently thanked her mother. Cooking wasn't Markie's strong suit, and Bryce didn't need to know that yet.

Just as she pulled out the second plate from inside the microwave, he reappeared in the kitchen.

"Smells great."

"Yeah, my mom is a pretty good cook. What would you like to drink? I have milk, iced tea, beer."

"Tea would be good. I can get it. Just point me in the direction of the glasses. What are you having?

"Milk."

Bryce poured the drinks as she set the plates on the table.

Markie sat across the small table from Bryce. Her brain reeled for any sort of conversation topics but nothing surfaced. The uncomfortable silence about killed her. No matter how hard she tried not to stare at the handsome man sitting across the table, she couldn't help herself. Part of her wanted to run around the table and kiss his worries away, but another part of her knew she shouldn't. She needed to stay focused and remember he was in her house for protection. Plus, she guessed he wasn't in the mood for conversation.

Bryce finished eating before she did but he remained at the table. Still wordless and uncomfortable. When she rose to clear the table he helped and loaded the dishwasher.

She needed to break this awful silence. "Do you want to watch television? I'm sure there must be a ball game on."

"For a while."

Markie flipped on the television and surfed the channels until she reached the first baseball game. "There's this one or I think the Brewers are on, too, tonight?"

He nodded as he sat on the opposite end of the couch from her. "The Brewers game if you don't mind?"

Super, he was a Brewers fan, too.

Outside of the announcers, there was no noise at all for the next hour.

After the game ended, Bryce turned toward her. "I think I'll just go to bed now."

"Me, too."

She rose and he followed suit. He wasted no time and headed for the hall. He paused at the doorway and looked back at her. "Thank you for letting me stay here. I do appreciate it."

"No problem."

He slipped into his room and she into hers.

She slid between the sheets and flipped off the light, but sleep didn't come. Rather, visions of the handsome man in the room across the hall infiltrated her mind. Those dark eyes of his sent her heart racing when she was lucky enough to capture his gaze. But, he never let her indulge too long. Fear?

Markie wondered if he was asleep yet. What would he do if she slipped in there? Would he let down his walls of defense and let her in? She sighed. Probably not. At least not yet. His actions let her know he fought it. Why though, she didn't know.

Flipping over, she fluffed her pillow, then looked at the clock. Two hours had passed, and she still hadn't fallen asleep. Her mouth was dry; perhaps a drink of water would help. She flung the covers back and rolled out of bed. Then she yanked the door open...and stepped through the doorway into one hundred percent lean muscle causing her to fall back. A large, warm hand wrapped around her forearm and steadied her against a hard, bare chest.

Heat from Bryce's body radiated into her. He stayed steady on his crutches, yet she teetered on her feet.

"You okay?"

She felt dazed.

"Markie?"

"Yeah. I didn't see you."

She pressed her palm to his pectoral. It was hard and hot, naked and soft. He inched back, now a bit unsteady on his crutches. The whole while she kept her hand in place. She wasn't done feeling him yet. In fact, her other hand wanted a feel, too, so she lifted that one and did the same as she edged her whole body closer to him.

"Markie, I can't."

Though he'd said those words, he made no move to push her away, sending her a different signal.

She slid her hands along his warm skin until they reached his neck, then she wrapped her fingers around him and pulled him toward her. He moved easily, crutches and all. His lips met hers in a light caress.

Bryce's large hands slid down her sides and then linked at the small of her back. He pulled her tightly

VALERIE J. CLARIZIO

to his body. Oh how she wanted his hands under her short, silky nightgown.

His tongue slid over the seam of her lips, and she parted them. He deepened the kiss. The slow strokes of his tongue increased in pace and explored farther in her mouth. His hands slid up the inside of her nightgown. The hot flesh of his palms scorched a path up her sides and he didn't stop until he eased them between their bodies to cup her breasts. Holy hell, his touch felt good.

Markie unlinked her fingers from around Bryce's neck and slowly skimmed them downward as he continued to kiss her senseless. *God, this guy can kiss.* She slipped her fingers under the waistband of his pajamas—

Bryce sprang back like she'd slapped him or something.

Even in the dark hallway, she could make out the fear in his eyes.

"Are you okay?"

He swallowed audibly.

She lifted her hand to touch his face and he leaned back. "Bryce?"

"I'm sorry, Markie. I…I just can't do this."

He looked so frightened, and his voice was unsteady; she wasn't sure what to say or do to not make matters worse. "It's okay."

He sighed and hung his head. "It's not you. It's me."

The old, *It's not you, it's me,* conversation irritated her, but only briefly, because in this case, she believed him. He had something going on. Something he needed to work through.

"Bryce, it's fine."

He lifted his head. "No, it's not. You're wonderful. You're smart and beautiful, and you deserve better."

"Better than what?"

After a long intake of breath, he let it out slowly. "Someone whole. You deserve someone whole."

This was all about his missing limb? Was he kidding?

"Are you referring to your leg, because if you are…"

"No…yes…well sort of."

"I can't believe you think so little of me."

"Excuse me?"

Markie planted her hands on her hips. "You think I'm so superficial I'd care about your leg?"

"No, this isn't coming out right." He ran his hand through his hair. "It's just the opposite. I think so much of you I don't want to burden you with my issues."

So much pain emitted from his gaze she debated just letting him off the hook and revisiting this uncomfortable conversation later, but she couldn't. She needed to know what bruised him so badly he'd push her away.

"I'm really not following you here. I've worked with you for two years. You seem to have your shit together, so I'm not sure what you are talking about."

Bryce inched back with his crutches and leaned against the wall. She was sure he was about to just end the conversation and go back to bed until he squared back to her, and looked her in the eyes. His serious gaze scared her. Was he sick or something?

"My leg was not my only injury caused when an IED exploded under my truck." He paused but continued to hold her gaze. "I had another injury and as a result—I may never be able to father children, and I just don't know…"

Her heart cracked in half for this man in front of her. This explained a lot. He pushed women away so he wouldn't have to deal with the real issue at hand. This also explained why he hung out with the Tiana's of the world. They weren't important to him, so he didn't have to worry about his issue.

Thrill snapped through her like a whip with the realization he really cared about her. He cared enough to tell her his deep, dark secret. He put himself out there to her. Going all in to see how she'd react.

Her heart hammered in her chest. This had to be the hardest thing he'd ever done.

Markie leaned in and pressed her lips to his. After a moment, he kissed her back. Long, slow, meaningful kisses. She'd take it as slow as he needed. Another layer to Bryce Hawk had been peeled back. *Success.* Good God he could kiss.

Chapter Ten

Bryce woke up with Markie curled under his arm. Her small, soft hand lay flat against his chest. Silky strands of her shiny, red hair tickled his chin. Her warm body molded perfectly to his, and that hint of cocoanut scent of hers nearly drove him insane.

They'd fallen asleep in the wee morning hours exhausted from kissing. She didn't push him for any more than what he was willing to give. He wanted to give much more than he did, but his will wasn't enough to overcome the fear—insecurity—that haunted him. What if he couldn't perform because of his injury? What if he couldn't satisfy her? A woman like her deserved a whole man. But, dammit, he couldn't seem to let her go last night. If ever there was a woman he wanted to try and make love with, it was her. But how could he be sure of himself without actually trying? Failing in front of Markie would be devastating.

She shifted and stretched, then lifted her head and fixed those piercing emerald eyes on him. Her tussled, red hair looked sexy as sin.

"Good morning."

Her lovely smile caused his heart to skip a beat. "Morning."

She shimmied up and pressed her lips lightly to his before glancing at the clock on her nightstand. He'd done the same moments ago to see how much time they had. Unfortunately, it was only minutes...or was that fortunate for him? Any more time in this bed with this woman would likely have him on top of her, and that, he wasn't ready to try yet.

She sighed. "I guess I have to get ready for work."

Markie rolled over and off the bed. He watched as she walked toward the master bathroom in a little nightgown that hardly covered her butt-cheeks. He wished it hadn't.

Once in the doorway, she stopped and looked back. "There's towels in the wall cabinet in the other bathroom, and anything else you should need."

"Thanks."

He waited for her to shut the door before he made a move for his crutches. Just because she knew about his leg didn't mean he was comfortable with her seeing its stump.

The shower started. The old Bryce, the man before the accident, would have been in that shower with her, lathering up that shapely body of hers.

Anxiety gripped his chest. The new Bryce couldn't.

He made his way to the bedroom he was supposed to have used, grabbed a change of clothes, the new toiletry bag, and slipped into the hall bathroom. Though the hot spray of the shower stung his burned and sliced up hands, the rest of his weary body welcomed the soothing water. The pain, however, triggered the memory as to why they were sore. Someone tried to kill him.

Who?

Once he and Markie got to work, they parted ways, she to her side of the building and him to his.

It didn't take but an hour for her and Captain Tomie to be knocking on his door. The expressions on their faces let him know it wasn't good news.

Hopefully, it wasn't a report in regard to another murdered property maintenance client.

"What's the matter?"

They stepped into his office and sat.

"We just got a call from a long-lost niece of Edwin Hulbert," Tomie blurted out "She's pissed. Evidently, he left everything to *you*. A pretty decent sized estate."

Bryce wheeled back from his computer and spun his chair to face the captain more directly.

"What? Me? Why?" The words came out in a stutter.

The man shrugged. "She was at the lawyer's office this morning, and that's what the man told her. Then he showed her the will. I take it the lawyer hasn't called you yet?"

He shook his head and gestured, palms in the air disbelievingly. "No, this is the first I'm hearing about it. But I still don't know why he would do that."

"Evidently, neither does she," Markie added. "The real problem is she is going to cause trouble for you."

"What do you mean?"

Markie and her superior exchanged a wary glance. "We looked at her social media accounts, and she's already spouting that you murdered her uncle for the inheritance."

His body tensed. "Is she crazy? So I'd murder someone for a few old cars and a homestead dating back to, I don't know, the early 1900s?"

Another mindful glance was exchanged between Markie and the captain.

"Evidently, Edwin saved every dime he'd ever made. According to his niece, the estate is worth almost a million dollars."

His heart thudded. *Holy shit.* No wonder his niece was pissed.

"This isn't looking good. She's going to make a stink about this and bring a lot more bad press to City Hall," Tomie said.

He was still speechless. *A million dollars.*

"Bryce?" Markie snapped her fingers.

He zoned in on her. "I had no idea. Where did this niece come from? I thought Edwin was alone."

"She's been estranged from him for a while. Her dad and uncle had a falling out decades ago. Her dad has since died. Judging from her social media posts, I'm guessing she's broke, and this was quite a blow to her. We're waiting to hear back from the lawyer," Markie informed.

Did he dare confirm his thoughts? "Is there any chance she knew of this before today...before my house blew up?"

Markie reached toward him and placed her comforting hand on his arm. "We're checking into that."

He blew out a breath and sighed. A week ago, everything was normal, on autopilot. And in such a short time, everything had gone to hell. He'd been questioned about two murders and had been nearly killed himself.

Well, not everything went to hell. There was the matter of the beautiful woman sitting across from him. At least he knew she believed he had nothing to do with the murders of Edwin and Sister Ann.

"So, this niece had a motive," Bryce stated.

"Yep. We've sent an officer to pick her up for questioning." Captain Tomie's phone buzzed, and he pulled it from the holder on his hip and glanced at the screen. "We gotta go." He looked at him. "You sit tight. We'll be back. Oh, and if you hear from the lawyer, patch him through to one of us. I'd like to find out more about Edwin's niece, or if he knows why the man didn't leave her anything in the will."

Captain and Markie got up. "Bryce, for your own safety, don't leave the building today," Tomie urged.

He nodded in understanding.

They left his office and Bryce dropped his head in his hands. *What in the hell?*

A few hours later, he got a call from Captain Tomie requesting he meet them at the police department office.

The receptionist buzzed him in, then he headed to the captain's office. Markie was already in there. The expressions on both their faces said it all. His pulse ratcheted up a notch.

"Who died now?"

Tomie cleared his throat. "Junior Willming. Looks suspicious."

Another one of his property maintenance accounts. The air drained from his lungs. This wasn't looking good; however, at least he had an alibi. He'd been at Markie's—all night—and in his office all day, with plenty of witnesses.

"How?"

"A broken handled spade buried in his chest."

Shit. Probably the same spade Junior threatened to hit him with the last time he was there. The one he'd grabbed to defend himself. His gut clenched. His fingerprints were going to be on that thing.

"Any leads?" Bryce asked.

Markie and the captain shared a somber glance.

"There was a piece of evidence left behind."

The lovely redhead squirmed in her chair. Her gaze hit the floor.

"What was it?" he asked, knowing it wasn't going to be good.

She slowly lifted her head. "Your business card was found in his mouth."

Anxiety swirled in his stomach. Was she really going to go there after what they'd shared the night before? Did she really think he was capable of something like this?

Wait. No. He was in the good. He'd been with her all night, and then at work all day.

Captain rested his elbows on his desk and leaned toward him. "We don't know for sure, and won't for a while, but it looks like Junior was killed several days ago."

There went his alibi. His heart thudded. Was he insinuating he was a person of interest in this murder? That's what it started to sound and look like. He glanced to Markie for reassurance that he was wrong and she believed he was innocent. Uncertainty— confusion emitted in her expression.

This can't be happening.

* * *

Markie watched as Bryce hung his head and walked back to his side of the City Hall building. All the ground she'd gained with him last night disappeared with one unsure look from her.

In her heart, she believed he was not the murderer, but the leads paved a clear path to him, and she'd seen people fooled time and time again by friends, relatives, and neighbors. Countless times she'd seen news interviews where someone commented, *"I can't believe so-and-so is a killer. He seemed like such a nice guy."* She, too, had been fooled by someone she loved and had committed to marry. Damn Conner Sunstrum with the golden hair and tongue that could talk a woman into anything—make a woman believe everything—showed her exactly how wrong she could be about a person. She'd been within one inch of marrying him when the truth surfaced.

The arrogant, cheating asshole.

Pain pierced her heart. She wanted to believe in Bryce, but a shadow of doubt had been planted in her brain, and it must have shown all over her face when he turned to her for reassurance. The hurt and disappointment in his eyes was one hundred percent on her, and it broke her heart. Yet she just sat there and let him walk away.

She'd been fooled by Conner. Was she being fooled by Bryce as well? If so, she was done with men forever.

Bile rose into her mouth. *Could* he be responsible for these murders? She hated herself for thinking such, but...

Captain cleared his throat. "You know he's not the murderer, right? This is clearly a setup. We just need to find out who's doing it before someone else gets killed, including Bryce."

"I know," she replied as she stiffened her spine to sit taller—more confidently in her chair.

"You look a little unsure."

Her efforts had failed. She just stared at him.

"This isn't my business, Markie, but, not all men are made from the same mold."

She straightened again and squared her shoulders. "I know."

He arched a brow. "Do you?"

"Yes," she said firmly trying to convince not only him, but herself.

"All right then. Let's focus. If this is a setup, who would have reason to do this?"

"For starters, that damn Tiana Bennett. She's obsessed with Bryce, and she gets pissed because he doesn't give her the time of day. Not to mention she stalks him."

"So, that explains why she would want to hurt or kill Bryce, but why would she murder the property maintenance violators?" Captain asked.

Good question. It didn't really make sense…unless, *hmm*. "A scenario comes to mind. If she can't have Bryce, she won't let anyone else either. Pin the murders on him and he goes to jail. Boom, no woman gets him then." She stood and paced the small room as the picture in her mind continued to develop. "She's unstable. Who knows what she could be thinking. Obviously, Bryce would be a believable suspect because of the nature of his relationship with the code violators."

Captain stood and wrote Tiana's name on the whiteboard hanging on the wall alongside his desk. "Who else?"

"Jeez, nobody else comes to mind. If not for the fact someone tried to kill Bryce, he looks guilty as sin. The victims were thorns in his side. They did nothing but cause him extra work. Yet I know he really liked Old Hulbert, but getting that inheritance only makes him look guiltier."

"What about any of the other property maintenance folks. Are there any more open cases? Perhaps we should look at those people. If they could pin something like this on Bryce, get him locked up, he wouldn't be able to keep hounding them about their own violations," Captain said.

Tomie picked up his phone and dialed Bryce's extension.

"Hey, Bryce. Do you have any more open property maintenance accounts? Uh huh... Okay... Thanks."

He hung up his phone and wrote Clyde Weston on the whiteboard.

Markie had forgotten about the shriveled up old drunk who spent most of his time at the bar and no time up-keeping his house, garage, and property.

"We'll go check on Clyde in a bit," Captain began. "Anyone else? Who does Bryce hang out with?"

"His dart team, but I think they're all friends and get along. He spends a lot of time with Lori Holloway, but she's the nicest person you'll ever meet," she stated before the memory surfaced of Lori tongue-lashing her in the bar the other night for giving Bryce a hard time. The woman had been angry. She'd never seen her like that before. Markie crossed an arm over her stomach, rested her elbow on it, and tapped her finger against her lips as she recalled the interaction.

"What is it? What are you thinking?" Captain asked raising a quizzical brow.

"I was just thinking about Lori Holloway. She got really angry with me about questioning Bryce last week."

He wrote Lori's name on the board.

"What would her motive be for killing anyone, or, more importantly, why Bryce? The woman obviously cares for him," Markie stated.

"Like you said about Tiana, if Lori can't have him maybe she thinks nobody should. Or, maybe she's doing it to help him by getting rid of his problem accounts."

"But what about Bryce? Why kill him?" Markie asked as she planted her hands on her hips.

"Maybe she blew up his house to throw you off the track. If she thinks you were accusing Bryce of the murders it would be a perfect way to save him. Think about it, maybe the explosion was just more than she'd bargained for, and she had just intended to send a message, not destroy everything. After all, it was set off in the garage, the farthest spot away from the master bedroom, and at a time when she knew he'd probably be in bed."

"Possible, I suppose."

"Let's keep going."

"Old Hulbert's niece," she offered. "Maybe she needed money bad enough to kill her uncle, thinking she would be named in the will since there are few to no other relatives. Maybe she found out about his will and wanted to knock off Bryce so he wouldn't inherit everything," Markie surmised.

"But why would she kill Sister Ann and Junior Willming?"

"Good question. Maybe there's more than one killer." She pointed at the board, "One for Bryce and one for the code violators."

Captain added Old Hulbert's niece to the board. "I think I know the answer to this question, but how long have you and Bryce been an item?"

Her pulse instantly ratcheted up a notch. "Huh?"

"You're going to tell me you're not a couple?" His brow arched again.

Though she didn't need to answer his question because she knew he knew the answer before he asked it, she did. "It was pretty much verified last night."

"What about Conner? Any reason he wouldn't want you and Bryce together?"

Just the sound of Conner's name caused her stomach to churn.

"The jackass is engaged to Sasha now so I doubt he cares who I'm with."

"But you dumped him, and an arrogant guy like him isn't used to that. They like to end things on their own terms. Or, if they do get dumped, they like to ensure the party that jilted them never stands a chance with anyone else. When was the last time you saw him?"

She shrugged. "Months ago."

"Did you talk to him then?"

"Briefly."

"Did he ask if you were seeing anyone?"

The lightbulb flipped on. "Yes, he did."

"And you said no, right?"

"Correct, because I wasn't at the time."

"So, at that point, there were no threats you'd be happy with someone else. I wonder if he found out about you and Bryce."

"But there was no me and Bryce before the murders. Actually, not before last night even."

"Seriously, Markie. First of all, we all saw it coming whether you two did or not, so likely, people outside of here did, too."

Markie would make sure to never play poker. Evidently, she didn't have the face for it.

"Secondly," the captain continued, "if your two murderer theory is correct, it could just be unusual timing. Coincidence. We need to consider that. Stranger things have happened."

She studied the list on the board:

Tiana Bennett
Clyde Weston
Lori Holloway
Edwin Hulbert's niece
Conner Sunstrom

Markie had her money on Tiana. In her opinion, that lady was pure evil. Clyde was too much of a drunk to pull it off. Lori was too nice—too much the innocent type. She supposed Old Hulbert's niece was a possibility, but she didn't know the woman, and they'd yet to locate her. As for Conner, she just couldn't see that. But hey, with her personal involvement with Conner and Bryce, the captain was probably seeing things more clearly than she was.

Captain's phone rang, and he picked it up. "Sure, I'll be right there."

He hung up the receiver and glanced at her. "Darrel from the hardware store is here. Says he may have information for us in regard to the explosion at Bryce's."

Her pulse quickened. A legitimate tip? Could this be the break they needed?

She followed her superior up front and buzzed Darrel through the doorway. Captain led the man to the small interview room equipped with an audio and visual recording system as she followed behind the two. She and Captain took a seat on one side of the cold, metal table and Darrel sat opposite them.

Darrel wove his fingers together and rested his shaky hands on the tabletop.

"Darrel, this is being recorded. Can you state your name and address for the record, please?" Captain asked.

The nervous man swung his gaze around the small room, pausing it at the ceiling-mounted camera before he returned it to them. There was no reason for the man to be so edgy. He was an upstanding citizen and Markie was certain whatever he told them would be the truth.

"Darrel Kratky. Four-six-two South Fourth Avenue."

"What information do you have?" Markie asked in a voice more eager than she'd intended. She drew in a calming breath. The man was already jumpy enough, she didn't need to make it any worse.

Darrel sucked his lips into his mouth and blew them back out with the breath he'd held. "During coffee time this morning at my store, Jim Lake from the sporting goods store said he sold Tiana Bennett some gunpowder Friday morning. He wondered what that crazy...excuse me, woman would want with gunpowder. Says he asked her and she said she needed it for reloading. Really, Tiana, reloading brass. I don't think so. Anyhow, Jim said he thought it was strange, but maybe it was for her dad or somebody else. Then Wade chimed in and said she'd been at the hardware store on Friday and purchased a small, metal pipe. Seriously, that little princess in a sporting goods store and hardware store just didn't make sense, so we got to thinking about it." Darrel paused and took a breath. "The explosion at Bryce's wasn't a pipe bomb was it?"

Adrenaline rushed her veins. *Darrel nailed it! That psycho, Tiana Bennett, tried to kill Bryce.*

Her purchasing those particular items for another use was just too coincidental. But did she kill the others, too?

One of the perks of a small town, everybody knew everybody's business. Or for some, it was probably a detriment. It certainly was looking that way for Ms. Bennett.

Impatiently, she waited as Captain Tomie asked Darrel a few more questions, and then told him to keep quiet about what he knew. She desperately wanted to run out the door, pick up Tiana and grill her. *Patience.*

Further solidifying his theory, Darrel confirmed Tiana's purchase with a copy of her credit card receipt. Excellent, he'd thought ahead by bringing the receipt.

Finally, Darrel left.

"I'll have Sargent Maxwell pick up Ms. Bennett from work."

Great, Maxwell was already in the field so he could get to Tiana quicker than if she did it herself.

Within five minutes, Maxwell had Tiana seated in the interview room. The woman looked relaxed, too relaxed. She leaned back in her chair and rested her arms on the table. Her long, red fingernails tapped on the tabletop as if she were annoyed—inconvenienced that she'd been hauled in.

"Ms. Bennett, did you kill Sister Ann, Edwin Hulbert, or Junior Willming?" Captain Tomie asked, cutting straight to the chase.

"Why would I do that? I don't even know those people," she replied matter-of-factly.

"I don't know why you would. Did you?"

"No."

"Do you know who did?"

The woman thought for a moment as a smirk consumed her face.

"Ms. Bennett, do you know who did it?" Captain asked again.

"No, but if I were you, I'd check with that bitch, Lori Holloway."

She had Markie's undivided attention now. Her superior's, too. Was this just an attempt to get them off her back and onto someone else?

The woman's smile stretched. No part of this was funny. Markie wanted to reach over and wipe that arrogant grin off her.

"You think Lori Holloway did it?" Captain asked.

"Could have." Her smug tone was beyond irritating.

"Why do you think that?"

"That lady is bat-shit crazy. She'd do anything for Bryce. Anything to get him, and anything to make his life easier. The funny part is, she's too stupid to know that no matter what she does for him, he's still not going to go out with a plain Jane like her." Tiana's gaze bore into Markie. "A man like Bryce, as good-looking as he is, requires a woman of beauty and sophistication."

"A woman like you?" Markie asked, trying to keep the defensiveness out of her tone.

Tiana smiled wickedly. How could she be so at ease—confident, when Markie was about to blow a gasket? Was she actually telling the truth, or some version thereof?

A strange theory started to play out in Markie's mind. Perhaps Lori was the murderer. Maybe she did it because she loved Bryce so much she wanted to make his life easier. Poor Bryce, these property maintenance issues were the pits. The guy was damned if he did and damned if he didn't see them through. The general public viewed him as a big meanie for picking on Sister Ann when he was just doing his job and concerned about her safety. As for Old Hulbert and Junior, it was kind of the same. But in their cases, some of the public sided with the city and wanted the properties cleaned up, while others wrote nasty comments on social media about the mean old city and the big bad property maintenance guy.

Markie stood in place, staring down at the conceited woman sitting at the table. She crossed an arm over her stomach swirling with anxiety, rested her elbow on her arm, and placed her chin to her hand. To others, she imagined she looked like the "Thinker" statue. How appropriate. She was thinking, trying to figure out how the attempt on Bryce's life fit in with her notion about Lori?

Theorizing further, keeping with Ms. Holloway being the killer of the property maintenance code violators, maybe when it started to look like Bryce was a leading suspect, Tiana stepped in to save the day for him. Making it look like he was on the killer's list would get him off the suspect list. Then, maybe she planned to leak out her suspicions about Lori being the murderer, which if it turned out to be true, she would then be successful in getting her out of her way when it came to Bryce. Only problem was Tiana wasn't smart enough to cover her tracks. That part threw up a red flag. To use her credit card to purchase a metal pipe and then use that pipe to blow up Bryce's house was blatantly stupid.

Markie pulled her chin from her hand and returned her gaze to Tiana. Another thought, was it probable she was the murderer and trying to set Lori up to take the fall so she could have Bryce to herself. This was a strong possibility as well—actually, more believable based on what Markie knew of the women and their general behaviors.

Her brain worked to process her theories and connections. If her theory was true about Lori being the killer of the property maintenance folks, why would she put Bryce's business card in Junior's mouth? The same question could be asked if Tiana were the killer. No matter which one was the killer, that business card maneuver would make him look blatantly guilty. Could that have been Tiana or Lori's plan? Make it so obvious he was the killer the police would think someone was setting him up? Thereby, shifting the focus off of him.

Perhaps some further questioning would shed some more light on this.

"Did you set off a pipe bomb in Bryce Hawk's garage?" the captain's question let Markie know he felt the same. More answers were needed.

"No."

"Where were you Friday night around midnight?" he asked.

"Home sleeping."

"Do you have anyone who can attest to that?"

"No, I was by myself. Sleeping. I live alone."

Liar. A woman like her doesn't sleep alone on a Friday night, and if she hadn't already found a partner by midnight, she certainly wouldn't be home since she had two-plus more hours of bar-time to find said partner.

"Did you get up at all that night and go anywhere?" Captain Tomie continued.

"No."

"Did you purchase gunpowder last week?"

Tiana's annoying finger tapping stilled. She looked to be contemplating how she was going to answer the question. Probably trying to figure out if she left a trail of that purchase. It was a small town. Likely, at least three people saw her in the store.

"Yes, for a friend for reloading. He asked me to pick it up for him." Her finger tapping started again.

The intimidating ex-Marine leaned toward her. "Does your friend use metal pipes for reloading?"

Her hand stilled again. "I'd like a lawyer," Tiana said flatly.

"I figured as much."

Markie followed Tomie out of the interview room and stood outside the door.

So, they had enough to hold Tiana but nothing but hearsay on Lori. Could they get her to come in voluntarily?

"I have an idea," Markie informed the captain.

"I'm listening."

"Let's have Bryce call Lori to get her to come into City Hall. When she gets here, we can let her know he is going to be charged with the murders. If Tiana is right, Lori may fess up to protect him."

"I see where you're going but that would be way too easy," Captain Tomie commented.

"I know, but it's worth a shot, right?"

He nodded. "We've got nothing to lose."

Bryce called Lori from his office phone. She easily agreed to come to City Hall without even asking why.

They watched and waited for her to put their plan in place. Within ten minutes, the woman parked in front of City Hall. She practically skipped into the building. An unstoppable smile covered her face. She buzzed by the reception desk and headed straight for Bryce's office.

They let Lori settle into the chair before they barged in with Sargent Maxwell.

Lori's eyes went wide. The blood drained from her face. She turned white as a ghost.

"Bryce Hawk, you're being charged with the murders of Sister Ann, Edwin Hulbert, and Junior Willming." Sargent Maxwell stated as he yanked Bryce out of his chair and read him his rights.

Lori sprang from her seat, and Captain Tomie placed his hand on her shoulder. "Stay put."

"But…"

"Quiet," Captain Tomie ordered.

Tears pooled in the shocked woman's eyes.

Maxwell handed Bryce his crutches and held him by the arm as he led him out of the office.

Bryce played along beautifully. The shocked look on his face when they barged in was priceless. He was just about out the door when Lori called out his name.

He glanced back at her. "It's okay. I didn't do it. I'll call my lawyer."

"Yeah, right," Markie huffed out.

Lori lunged toward her, but the captain held her back.

"He didn't do it! He didn't!"

Eagerly, she leaned toward the crying woman. "Really. That's not what the evidence suggests. We can place him at all three scenes, and he had an axe to grind with each one. Plus, he had a lot to gain by Edwin's death. He's guilty as sin."

Markie fixed her gaze on Bryce. "Three murders. You're never going to see the light of day from outside a prison fence again."

She swung her gaze back to Lori. The woman reached toward her, but the captain yanked her back.

"Lori, there's something I always wanted to tell you," Bryce said smoothly.

The woman's dark eyes softened. "Yes?" Her pining look was over-the-top.

He was adlibbing now? What was he going to say?

"I lo—"

"I did it! I did it for you, Bryce. I love you, too!" She planted her gaze on Markie. "He didn't do it. He didn't kill those people!"

Holy shit! A freaking confession. No way. Though they'd got exactly what they wanted, everyone other than Lori looked dumbfounded. Maxwell released Bryce and had Lori in cuffs in about three seconds. It was then it seemed to register with her what had happened.

She glanced back at the man she loved. Desperation was written all over her face. "Bryce?"

He shook his head.

The woman's body trembled. "No, no, no."

Maxwell read her her rights as they disappeared down the hall.

Bryce melted back into his chair.

He looked spent, exhausted, even a bit sick.

Empathy washed through her.

"What in the hell? Both of them?"

"Well, if it's any consolation, at least it appears both women were acting out...out of love, I guess," Captain Tomie stated.

"I feel sick. One killed people to make my job easier, and the other almost killed me to protect me from being a suspect?" Bryce recapped.

"That's the way it appears. But it is still possible Tiana intended to kill you to keep anyone else from having you. We'll keep working on that and flesh it out," Captain said, his tone sober as a judge.

That made it even worse.

"I kind of get Tiana, but Lori, it just doesn't seem right. She's always so kind and bubbly."

"People do strange and desperate things for all sorts of reasons important to them." The intuitive man placed his hand on Bryce's shoulder. "I know what you're thinking, and this isn't your fault. You are *not* responsible for this."

Markie tore her gaze from the men. She should be the one consoling him, yet, she let it to her superior. Why was she unable to come up with any words for him—the man she loved? *Loved?* Her stomach fluttered. Her pulse raced. Her palms perspired. Yes, she loved him.

Bryce was innocent. She knew it all along. Yet, her sense of judgment that had been tainted by her cheating ex-fiancé years ago kept her second-guessing herself, and held her at bay from her soulmate—Bryce.

Chapter Eleven

Markie was tied up with the investigation when Bryce left City Hall for the day. He let himself into her home with the key she'd given him and grabbed his stuff. Then he set the key on the counter with a note thanking her for her work on the case and her hospitality.

Staring at the note, he knew it was lame, but it was for the best. His eyes watered. *Cut the ties now. It will be easier this way versus when reality sets in and she figures me out—realizes the extent of my disabilities, and dumps me.*

He checked into a hotel downtown and flipped on the television. Completely drained, he sank into the faux leather chair.

All he could think about was the judgmental look Markie had given him earlier in the day, doubting his innocence. His chest hollowed. How could she after what they'd shared the night before?

He couldn't be with someone who doubted him like that. Her distrust hurt more than anything he'd ever endured before, including his injuries while in Afghanistan. She probably had no idea how that look pained him.

Bryce closed his eyes and rubbed his aching chest. Exhaustion consumed him.

A knock startled him out of his sound sleep. He glanced at the clock from the chair. Ten o'clock, he'd been out for over two hours. Who'd be knocking on his door at this hour? More importantly, who knew where he was? He knew who. Markie. He'd known he'd have to deal with her sometime, but he'd hoped it wouldn't be tonight. He wasn't ready.

Even through the peephole, her knotted jaw was easy to see. Her hands were ground into her hips. Smoke practically poured out of her flaring nostrils. He knew that note he left her was cold, but she deserved it for doubting him.

He pulled the door open. Said note was gripped in her hand, which was now only inches from his face.

"Really. *Hospitality*? Was that all it was to you?"

She stepped past him. He wasn't going to get out of this too easily.

"No, it wasn't to me. But apparently, that's all it was to you," he spat back.

Her eyes watered. He knew she knew exactly what he referred to, that look of doubt.

"I'm sorry." Her voice wasn't much more than a whisper.

"That's not going to cut it. The real you, your real feelings came out in that moment. You *doubted* me—didn't trust me. After what I'd shared with you. I put my full faith in you and poured out my soul. And you doubted me. You're as superficial as all the rest. You're all the same." His voice cracked.

In his entire life he'd never laid out so much depth to a person, and he felt like a fool even now, yet, he just kept pouring it on, telling her things he wished he hadn't…trusting she was a woman with whom he could share everything…a woman who could see beyond his disabilities and love him for who he was.

Moments ago, when he'd tongue-lashed her, his brain had begged him to stop, but his mouth kept going. It was like he knew he used that split second in time as a tool to push her away so he could revert to hiding behind the wall of defense he'd built years ago to guard him against the heartbreak that was destined to come when the full effects of his disabilities impacted her life.

Hurt swam in the tears clouding that emerald gaze pinned on him. Shards of pain sliced through his heart. He was such a coward to lay this breakup on her rather than assume responsibility.

Deep down, he knew she hadn't meant to judge—doubt him. He figured she did it because some part of her, some wounded part of her heart resurfaced—reopened during this trying time, causing her to doubt him, unconsciously push him away, keep him at arm's length.

What a duo we are.

Maybe neither of them were ready for anything more yet the desire delightfully swirling in every cell in his body begged him to reconsider. His extremities shook with excitement. Just as quickly, that usual, dreadful shadow of doubt froze the exhilarating rush of adrenaline in his veins. *Use your common sense, Bryce. It will never work.*

She reached out to him, and he backed up.

"Okay then. I'll just go."

Like an idiot he let her.

The door clicked shut, and he stayed frozen in place. Chicken-shit. Ball-less.

Ha. Ball-less. He laughed hysterically at his own joke even though it wasn't funny. At that moment, he realized the woman he just let go knew his deepest, darkest secret, yet she still came knocking on his door. His dad had been spot-on. She *was* the right woman for him.

She had knocked on his door *knowing*. If or when the time came that his nightmares held true, and he couldn't father children... he swallowed hard—or satisfy her. They'd work through it. She'd proven over and over she would be understanding and patient.

Much unlike the way he'd been moments ago.

He yanked the door open prepared to go forward when Markie suddenly sprang through, poking at his chest.

"I call bullshit."

"Huh."

"What you said is absolute *bullshit*. You don't mean it. It's just your way to make it about me and my issues with trust, rather than you taking ownership of your fear. Your own issues and not dealing with them. I'm not going to let you lay this on me," Markie spat.

She hitched her chin up. Her bright green eyes sparked a challenge.

All he could do was smile at her.

She'd hit the nail on the head, and he knew it. She was right. He'd heard second-hand about her cheating fiancé, he knew her story, and though the last thing he wanted to do was hurt her, he did just that a moment ago by using her fears as a tool to hide from facing his own. Just like she'd said.

Markie ground her hands on her hips. "Why are you smiling? This isn't funny."

"No, it's not."

Bryce dropped his crutches, wrapped his arms around her, and pulled her tight to his body. He crushed his mouth down on hers in a hot, needy, unbridled kiss. He put absolutely everything he had into it. Years of built-up need and desire flowed through him and poured out.

The incredible woman in his arms met him with an equal amount of passion—lust. Quite the desperate pair they were. Lips locked, tongues caressed, hands roamed. Clothes fell to the floor.

He was going to be okay. She was going to be satisfied. He'd never let her down. Physically or emotionally. She was the right woman for him.

*****

Dear Reader,

Thank you for reading THE CODE ENFORCER, the first book in the Crime & Passion Stalk City Hall series. I hope you enjoyed Markie & Bryce's story.

The next book in the series is A BRUSH WITH DEATH. Will Ben and Cori be as lucky as Markie and Bryce were by escaping the claws of death and finding their happily ever after?

Don't miss out! You can find links to all of my books on my website: https://valeriejclarizio.com/

If you'd like to be the first to find out about my new releases or book deals, please sign up for my newsletter.

https://valeriejclarizio.com/newsletter-signup-page/

I love connecting with my readers so feel free to drop me a note anytime at valclarizio@yahoo.com or keep in touch with me on Twitter @VClarizio or join my Facebook group Clarizio's Cronies.

If you'd like to support me, please leave a review. You are the reason I write and I sincerely appreciate you!

Best,
Valerie

About the Author

Valerie Clarizio lives in romantic Door County Wisconsin with her husband and two spoiled cats. She loves to read, write, and spend time at her cabin in the Upper Peninsula of Michigan.

She's lived her life surrounded by men, three brothers, a husband, and a male Siamese cat who required his own instruction manual. Keeping up with all the men in her life has turned her into an outdoors enthusiast, of which her favorite activity is hiking. While out on the trails, she has plenty of time to conjure up irresistible characters and unique storylines for her next romance novel.

Connect with Valerie

Website/Blog: https://valeriejclarizio.com/
Newsletter: https://valeriejclarizio.com/newsletter-signup-page/
Bookbub: https://www.bookbub.com/authors/valerie-j-clarizio
Facebook:
https://www.facebook.com/Valerie.Clarizio/
Facebook Street Team:
https://www.facebook.com/groups/clariozioscronies/
Twitter: https://twitter.com/VClarizio
Instagram:
https://www.instagram.com/valerieclarizio/
Pinterest: https://www.pinterest.com/valerieclarizio/

Valerie J. Clarizio's Other Titles:

The Nick Spinelli Romance Mystery Series
Covert Exposure, a Nick Spinelli Mystery, novella 1
Craving Vengeance, a Nick Spinelli Mystery, novella 2
Crazed Reckoning, a Nick Spinelli Mystery, novella 3

Romantic Suspense Titles
Taken by Surprise
Unforeseen Obsessions
Plan Interrupted

Chandler County Series
Missing the Crown Jewels
Missing out on Life

Crime & Passion Stalk City Hall Series
The Code Enforcer
A Brush with Death

Time Travel Romance Titles
Time WARped
Destiny Reclaimed

Contemporary Romance Titles
Family Forever

Short Story Titles
Love Thaws a Frozen Heart

Love on the Door County Peninsula Series
Talia & Ryan's Story
Jess & Sam's Story